ChangelingPress.com

Morgue/Deacon Duet
A Bones MC Romance
Marteeka Karland

Morgue/Deacon Duet
A Bones MC Romance
Marteeka Klarland

ISBN: 978-1-60521-937-0

Publisher:
Changeling Press LLC
315 N. Centre St.
Martinsburg, WV 25404
ChangelingPress.com

Printed in the U.S.A.

Editor: Jean Cooper
Cover Artist: Marteeka Karland

The individual stories in this anthology have been previously released in E-Book format.

Table of Contents

Morgue (Iron Tzars MC 11)
A Bones MC Romance
Marteeka Karland

My need for vengeance knows no limits. I will make everyone who hurt my woman pay.

Dorothy: Spring Break turned into my worst nightmare. Drugged and held against my will, the brutality I witnessed seems too horrible to be real. Unable to escape, unable to do anything other than await my fate, I nearly gave up hope. Then *he* burst through the door like an avenging angel. My very own angel of death.

Morgue: I'm a straight-up killer. It's what I've trained for my entire adult life. I got my road name because I've put more men in the morgue than all my brothers combined. So when we rescue a group of women being held by human traffickers, I did what I do best. I killed. But not for all the women we rescued. For *her*. Dorothy. My very own angel of mercy. Now that I have her, I'll do anything to keep her. I just hope she can accept what I am and not condemn my soul to hell.

Chapter One

Dorothy

Moans from other women in the shitty little shack filled the air. I knew the feeling. My head throbbed and every muscle in my body ached. The rooms were paper thin so we could all hear the screams of the others around us. The cruel laughter of men. The frightened whimpers of the women. And girls. I had absolutely no idea where I was or how long I'd been there, but I knew it wasn't Kansas.

"*Levántate, perra. Afuera.*"

"I don't understand." It wasn't a new thing. And I'd paid for not knowing Spanish more than once since I'd been taken.

"*¡Ahora!*" The guy knew I didn't understand. It felt like he took pleasure in the fact I didn't understand so he could single me out. I shrank back, trying to make myself smaller in the face of the brutality I knew was about to happen. He lunged forward and backhanded me before grabbing my arm and shoving me out of the tiny room I shared with five other girls.

I hit the floor, my knees slamming onto the hard dirt. Pain shot from my knees up my thighs, and I cried out. When I tried to get up, the guy kicked me in the side. My head spun with all the sudden movements. I thought it was also some kind of lingering effect of the drugs they kept shooting me full of. They did it to everyone who fought. Unless they wanted us to fight. I got dosed often.

"*Perra estúpida,*" he muttered. I got the "stupid" part, and I could only assume the other was "bitch," but it could have been anything. The kick knocked the breath out of me and sent pain exploding through my ribs. I groaned but knew better than to make too much of a fuss. Noise drew attention I didn't want. Attention meant someone was about to hurt me worse than I already was.

"¡*Escuchen!*" The big brute swept his hand through the air, obviously wanting everyone's attention. He spoke in a string of rapid-fire Spanish I didn't understand. I was pretty sure something horrible was about to happen and I sincerely hoped it didn't have anything to do with me. I'd been here maybe a week. Seemed like longer. I was surprised this guy or the men and women with him hadn't done more than terrorize me or the other women. Though I was sure the qualifier "yet" needed to be added. There was no way they'd brought us here for tantalizing conversation. Though I'd been smacked around a lot and was covered in bruises, they hadn't seriously harmed me. Again, there was that fucking qualifier hanging over my head.

I crawled very slowly to the wall where the other women were, trying not to make sudden moves so he didn't bring his focus back to me. The one thing I knew for sure -- in spite of the language barrier -- was that I absolutely did not want any of these men to focus on me for too long.

All the women around me were whimpering and trembling, looking as terrified as I felt. A few looked like they might have checked out and I didn't blame them. If I knew how, I probably would too. Fighting back didn't seem like the smart thing to do if I wanted to live. While I knew there were fates worse than death, I wasn't ready to contemplate them just yet. I was sure, at some point, I'd have to face that decision, and I wasn't looking forward to it.

More rapid-fire Spanish followed as one of the other men dragged a young woman down the hall and tossed her to the ground so she skidded several feet before rolling to her knees with a whimper. She'd been beaten, one side of her face swollen. I hadn't seen her before, but, given the track marks on her arms and how badly she'd been beaten, I was certain she'd attempted to escape. They'd likely dosed her as much as they'd dosed the rest of us when we got out of line. Only, this time, I got the impression this guy was done taking shit.

"*Esto es lo que les pasa a las perras que no me obedecen. Si no me obedeces, esto te pasará.*"

I didn't understand. But I didn't have to. The next thing I knew, he'd drawn out a machete. The girl screamed and tried to scramble back only to be held in place by two more men. A third helped them wrestle her to the ground onto her back. Once they had her down, the third guy held her legs at the ankles. There was a *whoosh* as the blade cut through the air and came down on her right thigh.

Blood arced when he raised the machete and brought it down again on the same leg. It took three more tries before he hacked her leg off and started on the other one. Everyone screamed, myself included. When anyone turned away, there were men to force them to turn back. And watch.

Before he got her second leg hacked off, the woman was unconscious. There was blood splatter everywhere, but once a limb was completely severed, the bleeding slowed dramatically. Still, the men tied tourniquets above the stumps.

I'm sure I was one of the women screaming. If I was, though, I had no memory of it. All I could process was a young woman getting her legs chopped off.

"*Esto es lo que sucede cuando intentas escapar.*" He spat on her. "*Una puta sin piernas es más fácil de follar.*

¿Sí?"

I stared at the unconscious woman. Though he hadn't killed her outright, I was sure she wouldn't last long. One of the men grabbed her wrist and dragged her out of the room, leaving a trail of blood as he went.

As I watched, one of the men approached me with an evil smirk on his face. "In case you're wondering," he said in thickly accented Spanish, "He said this is what happens when you try to escape, *Americana.*" He grinned. "And a whore without legs is easier to fuck." He snorted a laugh. "I happen to agree. So, I'm really hoping you try to escape too."

I barely held back a sob of despair. I knew he was trying to elicit a response from me, likely to give him a reason to hit me. There were some of us who tried to fight back when they came for us, but we were always overpowered. So far, all they'd done was beat me, but most of the others had been brutally raped and I knew that's what they were building up to. This was a whorehouse of sorts. Only, the women didn't get paid. The men who "owned" us did. A place where we were all used and trafficked.

The guy backhanded me when I didn't respond to him. I fell back with a cry, covering my head with my arms and whimpering.

"Don't worry, bitch. You won't suffer long. I doubt you make it a month once we start breaking you in." He gave a bark of laughter before kicking me.

My head swam from both the blow to my face and the remaining drugs in my system. More men crowded us in the tiny corridor only to shove us into various rooms. There were five more women in the room I landed in. Three filthy mattresses lay on the floor and a bucket sat in one corner for us to relieve ourselves. That's the way it had been since I'd been here.

The next thing was the men coming to shoot us full of whatever drug they were using. I suspected it was heroin. A couple of the girls screamed while the other three complied easily. Probably because they were addicted or figured it was better to endure whatever happened next while blissfully numb than stone-cold sober. I understood. While I couldn't put up much of a fight this time, I wanted to. Desperately. I hadn't given up hope of getting out of here alive. Not really. Not yet. But I wasn't too ashamed to admit I was fucking close.

A man held my arm while another jabbed a needle into my arm at the bend of my elbow and pressed the plunger. The pain of the dull needle sinking into my arm was soon replaced by a sickening euphoria. My eyes glazed over and my body went limp. I was still conscious, but... detached.

That was when one of the men shoved me onto a mattress and pulled at my clothes. He was breathing heavily and talking in Spanish, but I got the gist of what he was saying. He was going to fuck me. I caught the word *"Americana"* and figured he was taking bragging rights by fucking the American woman. They all looked at my blonde hair and blue eyes, going so far as to pry my eyes open and touch my eyeball, like a child testing if something was real. Maybe they thought I had contacts or something. Many of them felt my hair, fisting it and mimicked wrapping it around their cocks. I imagined far worse was going to happen shortly.

I whimpered but couldn't even form words to tell the guy to stop. Not that it would have done any good. I batted at him weakly, but he didn't seem to notice much less even acknowledge I was trying to fight him off.

Once he had me naked from the waist down, the guy crawled on top of me, pressing me into the filthy mattress. He reached between us and freed his cock. I could feel the head of it touching me. I shuddered, gagging as I pushed at him weakly.

"No!" I tried to shout the word at him, but it was a whisper at best. Just as he was about to penetrate me, there was a huge *bang* and the door splintered, throwing pieces of wood all around the room. I was sure some were embedded in my skin, but I still couldn't do more than try to roll away from the man on top of me.

He shouted, pushing himself to his feet. Once his weight was off me, I crawled as best I could to the corner of the room and tucked myself into a ball. It was all I was capable of. I couldn't even cry. Oh, tears poured freely from my eyes, but I didn't have the strength to sob out my fear and frustration.

I thought there were screams all around me, not only in this room but in others nearby, but it was hard to tell. The more I tried to move, the more the room spun. Somewhere in the background of all that, and the ringing in my ears, I knew a fight raged. Was it more men coming to chop off the legs of someone else? Oh, God!

Then someone grabbed at my arms. I was helpless to stop them. I thought I was even more groggy than I had been when I was about to be raped. Whatever drug they'd given me had started to take hold. It was only the adrenaline coursing through my veins that kept me conscious.

"Hold on, honey. We're gettin' you outta here."

"P-Please..." I managed to gasp out between embarrassing whimpers. "D-don't h-hurt me." It was a pitiful attempt at begging, and I knew it. But I had nothing else. No energy. No clarity of mind. I didn't know what to say to appease this man.

"No one's gonna hurt you. I've got you. Takin' you back to the States. You're safe." The man's voice was deep and rough. It wasn't soothing in the least. In fact, it was nearly as frightening as the voices of the men who held me prisoner here. The only difference was I understood what this guy was saying. At the moment, he was saying all the right things, but what if that was to get me to cooperate?

"No... D-don't h-hurt m-me..." I could barely breathe. My heart pounded and my guts churned. If I'd had anything in my stomach I would have puked. My insides rebelled at being moved. The way my head swam didn't help matters either.

He didn't say anything else, but it wasn't long until a harsh wind blew into my face. There was no rain, but it reminded me of home when a tornado was about to hit. There might not be rain, but the gale carried projectiles and blew so hard it would have probably knocked me off my feet. I vaguely remembered hearing the howling wind but had been too terrified to really notice.

"We've got to get to the airfield!" a man beside us yelled. "I doubt even Deke can take off in this shit!"

"We may need to find shelter and wait it out!" The guy carrying me had to yell to be heard over the roaring of the wind.

"Smoke says he's hoping for a break in the weather. Something about the outer bands having an uneven edge? I don't know." I was able to open my eyes and focus just as an old, light-colored pickup of some sort pulled up and skidded to a halt.

"Get 'em in the back of the Humvee. Not too

comfortable, but it's protection from the wind. Rain's comin' too."

The next thing I knew, I was being shoved into the back corner of an enclosed vehicle. I thought the same man had hold of me, but wasn't sure. I looked up at his face, trying to see through the haze over my vision and in the dim light.

He wore a combat helmet, as well as a dark T-shirt and a bulletproof vest over his shirt. A full beard obscured his lower face. Tattoos covered his arms and crept up one side of his neck which glistened with sweat. I could feel his strength where I lay against him as the truck jolted forward. About the time we took off, rain started coming down. There were a couple of small windows, one of them close to me. Water distorted the view as rain pelted against the glass, though it was possible my vision was simply too fuzzy to see. Combine that with the jostling of the vehicle as they sped over the rough terrain, and I had no idea what was actually going on outside.

The guy took a bottle of water from someone and twisted the top off it. "Can you drink for me?"

Was he kidding? I wanted water almost more than I wanted my freedom. I nodded, and he placed the mouth to my lips and tilted the bottle gently. I tried to gulp it down, but he forced me to go slow. If I'd been strong enough, I'd have grabbed the bottle and done it myself, but I couldn't make my arms move. It felt like they were weighted down, or tied. No matter how hard I tried to move them, I couldn't seem to lift more than a finger.

"Take it slow, honey. I don't want you to get sick."

"More," I croaked.

"I know. I get it. Let me help you so you don't

get too much at once."

It wasn't like I had much choice. My body felt like it weighed a ton. My eyelids too. But, God, I was so fucking thirsty!

The truck bounced sharply. Every time the guy pressed the lip of the bottle to my mouth, my whole being focused on getting as much water as he'd let me have.

When we hit a bump, water splashed over my lower face and dribbled down my chin and neck. It felt like heaven. I knew I should be worried about this. About getting caught and having my legs chopped off -- and worse -- but all I could concentrate on was that delicious, invigorating water.

Shots rang out and the other women in the truck screamed. I probably would have too if I hadn't been concentrating on the water. More gunfire -- this time, it came from us. The men in the truck were shooting back. The man holding me shifted so I slid down to the floor of the vehicle. He tucked a blanket around me before shouldering the rifle and pulled out his own handgun. When I whimpered, his gaze landed on me again.

"I'll be right back. Just gonna teach these fuckers a lesson." He waited until I nodded at him before he moved. Things got a little hazy then as dizziness nearly pulled me under. Somehow, he slid a window open, stuck out his rifle, and started shooting.

I watched in silence as the other men brought out assault-style rifles and fired at the vehicle -- or vehicles -- following us. They spoke quietly and to each other. I could hear their voices but couldn't understand what they were saying. The ringing in my ears, from both the drug I'd been given and the report of the gunshots, made it hard to focus on anything else, other than the water bottle in my hand.

With my man not holding me back anymore, I gulped greedily at the water until the bottle was empty. Then I thought about the other women and was instantly ashamed and horrified at my actions.

"I'm so sorry," I croaked out as I met the gaze of another woman in the vehicle beside me. "I didn't even offer."

"We all have water." Her voice was as rough as mine but thickly accented with Spanish. "And no one else did either." She gave me a small smile. "Is what happens when we're all turned into animals." She wasn't wrong.

Shots continued to ring out. With every bump and slide of the truck, we were all jostled around. I tried to brace myself, but it was impossible. Even though I felt a little better after drinking the water, the drugs in my system still made it nearly impossible to focus, zapping what little strength I might have had.

The truck slid sideways before coming to a stop. Someone opened the back of the vehicle, and the door was shoved wide open. There was muffled cursing as well as more gunfire as wind and rain whooshed in, instantly soaking us.

Men shouted. Guns fired. Women screamed. All I could do was sit there and await my fate. The man who'd carried me out and fed me water looked back over his shoulder and our gazes collided. His was ice-cold, his features carved from stone. He reminded me of the men who'd held us captive, the men they'd rescued us from. There was that kind of intensity and cruelty there. For the first time since he'd carried me out, I wondered if I might not have landed in as bad a situation as I'd just come from.

He held my gaze for a couple of seconds before

giving me a slight nod and turning back to the fight.

And just like that, my fate was sealed. I might not know what awaited me when we got out of this mess, but I knew I'd forever look back at this moment and know I was alive -- for good or ill -- because of this man. Whether I lived or died in the back of this truck, filthy, half dead, and drugged to the gills, would depend on this man's will. Because he was a warrior. *The* warrior. If he decided I was worthy, he'd keep me safe. If not? Well. He was the one to pull me out of hell. I'd trust him to get me across the gates.

With that last thought, I let the blackness of a drug-induced sleep have me. It wasn't like it mattered much anyway. If death was coming for me, maybe it was better not to see it coming.

Chapter Two
Morgue

"Motherfuckers." I muttered the curse as I fired off another round. This one got the driver of the truck. The vehicle drifted sharply off the road and into a huge rock. Men standing in the back firing over the cab flew forward and into the sand of the surrounding area. "Clutch! We got 'em! Hard stop!"

Clutch, our road captain, stopped the truck at an angle so we'd have a better defensive position if these bastards were in any shape to fight back. The three of us in the Humvee with the women jumped out and moved quickly toward the wrecked vehicle.

Three men had been thrown from the wrecked vehicle. Each man I passed, I shot in the head twice. Just to make sure. The driver of the truck groaned. Deacon reached him first. When Deacon didn't immediately shoot the bastard, I raised my gun to do the job.

"Morgue, stop!" I ground my teeth in frustration as Brick, the vice president of Iron Tzars, shoved my gun hand upward to prevent the kill. "We need to get some answers from someone in this fucking cesspool. With everyone else dead, he's nominated."

"Needs to die," I bit out.

"He will." Brick put himself between me and the bastard. I growled and tried to peer around Brick, but he was a wide son of a bitch. "Just not before he tells us who else is involved in this ring." When I still tried to get around him, Brick slammed the palm of his hand against the middle of my chest, forcibly making me stop. "Morgue," Brick said warningly. "Back the fuck off. Now."

I grunted before turning away and stomping

back to the truck. We'd only managed to rescue five women from that place. Of the three other women in those rooms, two were already dead and the last one died when we tried to move her. One of the five we had in the truck looked like she might be barely in her teens. If that. All of them were in pretty bad shape, but the woman I'd carried out seemed to be the worst. I calculated the odds she'd make it back to Evansville at about thirty percent.

As I approached the truck, one of the women gave a strangled cry. There was a commotion and a lot of thumping before there was another yelp.

"You're all right. You're all right." Stitches, the club doctor, tried to soothe his patient. When I reached the truck and poked my head under the tarp, I saw him hold out a bottle of water to the woman I'd helped earlier. She looked decidedly more awake but more than a little terrified. "Just took the edge off the drug they gave you."

"What the fuck'd you do to 'er?" The demand came from me before I even truly realized I was going to speak.

Stitches glanced over his shoulder at me with a raised eyebrow. "Gave her some Narcan. They had her doped up. Bit harsh when it hits."

"Then why'd you do it? She was breathin' on her own and shit."

The look Stitches gave me had my back up. It was the look a doctor gave an armchair quarterback when being questioned about something medical. "Several reasons. First and foremost, because it's none of your Goddamned business. I'm the fuckin' doctor. Not you. You don't get to question me."

I ground my teeth together as I holstered my pistol. I'd already slung my rifle around my neck and secured it to my vest. I needed both weapons at the ready in case there were more of these fuckers we'd missed. The woman sat up, her breathing harsh and ragged. Her eyes were wide open, and she'd started to sweat. "She still looks like crap, but she looked better before you started workin' on her. What the fuck, Stitches?"

He huffed out an annoyed breath. "Either go looking for more of those bastards or shut up and get in the damned truck."

"Your bedside manner needs a little work," I groused, but I climbed in the back of the Humvee. I heard a couple more shots around us, then Deacon and Smoke hopped back in and Crush took off. The woman screamed, swatting at Stitches and looking around wide-eyed.

"Ohmigod! What happened? Holy shit!" She looked at Stitches, but her gaze darted around like she was trapped and looking for someone to pounce on her.

"Just a little take-me-down." Stitches was only half paying attention to her as he fiddled with her IV, injecting something into it that seemed to help her. She didn't have that drugged look about her she had before, but she wasn't jumping out of her skin. "There. Try to take some deep breaths. The medicine I gave you will wear off in thirty minutes, so don't fight it when it happens."

"I don't want to be like that again. I need to have my wits about me." She looked terrified. As she should be.

"I know and I'm sorry. I'll get you more as soon as we get on the plane, but I've only got a limited supply, so unless I'm afraid you're gonna lose your airway I'm gonna have to let it wear off. Just needed to make sure there was nothing that needed immediate medical attention. Now, look at me." She closed her eyes and took a deep breath before letting her breath out slowly. When she opened her eyes, she was steadier. "Good. Now. What's your name?" Stitches spoke kindly but firmly, taking charge without being bossy or abrasive.

"Dorothy."

"Good. That's good. Where you from, Dorothy?"

"I'm, uh…" She cleared her throat. "Liberal, Kansas."

Stitches chuckled. "Really. Dorothy Gale's hometown?"

"Yeah. But my last name ain't Gale. And though I like the book and the movie, any Wizard of Oz references will be met with swift and brutal retaliation." Her eyes were clearer than they had been, but her words were still slightly slurred. She'd definitely been drugged, and was still fighting despite the medication to reverse it.

Stitches gave the woman what was probably a charming smile. I wanted to kill the smug bastard for looking at her. "Not a one. I swear."

Dorothy gave him a half grin that didn't look like she meant it. It was the only reason I was gonna let Stitches live. "Not many people can keep from it. I mean, if I only had a brain…" She glanced around but quickly closed her eyes and groaned. "Where's the guy who pulled me out of that hellhole?"

That's right, Stitches. She asked for me. Not you. And fuck you anyway. I cleared my throat. "Me," I said. "I got you out."

She looked up at me, her lips parting. She nodded. "Yes. It's you." Her breath started coming quicker and tears formed in her eyes. "Are you real?"

Her voice shook, and I wasn't really sure what to say or do to make it stop. And as glad as I'd been when she asked for me, I'd give up her recognition if she just wouldn't cry. Yeah. I was fucked.

"Last time I checked," I muttered. The sarcastic reply just tumbled off my lips. As a rule, I was pretty close-lipped, but that just meant my brain was able to keep up with my mouth. I thought plenty that needed to stay in my head, but occasionally it would slip. Like in situations of extreme duress. Like when faced with this woman's tears. And it wasn't women's tears in general I was averse to. In my experience, women used tears as a way to manipulate. No. I knew in my heart I'd do anything... anything... to prevent this woman from crying.

To my surprise, she let out a small bark of laughter. "I guess that's all I could ask for." The tears still came, but she managed a genuine smile. "Thank you so fucking much."

"You're welcome." I cleared my throat and looked away, but settled myself close to her so we sat side by side.

She took a deep breath once again before looking at Stitches again. "Other than several beatings, I wasn't hurt. They kept me drugged most of the time, but they hadn't raped me yet. Not like some of the others." She shivered and I glanced around. Most of the other women were either passed out or asleep. One gave her a steady look before nodding her head at Dorothy. I wasn't sure if it was a show of solidarity or just an acknowledgment of the shared trauma, but Dorothy nodded back.

"All right, then. What hurts the most?"

"My ribs." She groaned and raised her shirt so Stitches could see her side. "Bastard kicked me just before everything went to hell. Other than that, just the drugs. Pretty sure it was heroin or some kind of opioid."

"It was. The Narcan's all the proof I need of that. Only question is what else did they give you? Probably nothing else since you responded so well."

"Well, I guess that's something." She sat back and I hooked my arm around her. If she noticed, she didn't mind. Just lay against me with her head on my shoulder like she fucking belonged there.

"Yeah." Stitches grinned. "I suppose it is. You OK with that buffoon all up in your shit?"

She nodded. "Yeah. He feels safe."

"All right, then. It won't be too long until the Narcan wears off. Don't fight it. I'm watching over you, and Morgue there won't let anything happen to you."

Her gaze snapped to mine, and I decided Stitches would indeed have to die. "Morgue?"

I opened my mouth to respond, but Stitches beat me to it. "Yep. You heard right, little girl. His name's Morgue."

"Why's that?"

I shot Stitches a look that let the bastard know he was dead meat. "Just is."

Stitches snorted. "Because your man there has sent more people to the morgue than all of us combined."

To my surprise, Dorothy gave me a slow nod. "Good. You won't let those bastards take me back, then." She said it like it was a foregone conclusion, but I could see the question and vulnerability in her eyes.

"No, honey. I won't let them near you."

"Good, 'cause my head's startin' 'ta spin 'gain."

"I've got you. Just hang on to me. I'll keep you

safe."

Instead of responding, Dorothy closed her eyes and gave in to the drug invading her system. I looked up at Stitches. "When this is over and they're all safe, I'm gonna kill you."

Stitches shrugged. "Get in line. Pretty sure there are a few in front of you. Besides, hearing you're a crazy serial killer wannabe seemed to be exactly what she needed."

"I'm not a serial killer. Everyone I killed needed killin'."

"OK. I'll give you that. Still helped so I ain't sorry. And I ain't takin' it back." He turned his attention to another one of the women. I turned mine back to Dorothy.

I glanced down to see her hand clutching my thigh even in her drugged state. She wasn't completely out of it, I didn't think, but she was in and out if the way her eyes opened and shut occasionally was any indication.

I settled her closer before checking my gun once more. I'd already done so, but not only had we just killed everyone in the rat trap where we found these women, but we were in Mexican territory. We'd taken women the Cartel saw as their property. If it was discovered before we were safely away, we'd be in a fight all the way back to Evansville.

"How are the others?"

Stitches shook his head. "One won't make it. One will be touch and go. Dorothy and the other two should be fine physically unless there's internal damage I can't see. One of them got hit in the head pretty hard, but she's responding appropriately. At least for now."

"They drugged too?"

"Yeah. Either they weren't dosed as hard, or they've been dosed so often they're becoming resistant. They're a little woozy but not as much as Dorothy. I doubt she's been here as long as the others. Not as banged up either."

The Humvee continued to speed over the rough terrain, the wind and rain pounding the vehicle mercilessly. I glanced down at the sleeping woman against me. She was battered, beaten, and filthy as hell. But I'd never seen a more striking female. I wasn't too proud to admit I loved the way she trusted me, even knowing I was a killer. Maybe Stitches was right. Maybe she felt safe because I was a killer.

The Humvee skidded to a halt with a jolt. "Fuck." I moved to the back of the enclosure and looked out the window. The rain was coming down too hard for me to see if we'd picked up a tail, but we weren't being shot at.

"We're here." Clutch threw the vehicle in park and got out, slamming the door behind him. I followed out the back, hurrying around the truck to cover Clutch. He headed toward a battered hangar where Deke was supposed to be waiting for us. He was on loan from Bones MC in Kentucky. While I didn't like depending on someone outside the Tzars for our extraction, Sting vouched for this guy, so I'd give him the benefit of the doubt. Supposedly, there wasn't any kind of aircraft the bastard couldn't fly.

I trotted to catch up with Clutch. The hangar wasn't much more than an oversized carport. The sides came down about halfway from the top to the ground, but it was rusted out in places and did little to protect the chopper Deke had brought for the extraction. The man stood just under the canopy next to the UH-1Y Venom helicopter we were supposed to exfiltrate with.

Fucking big-ass bird to hide. The military aircraft was owned by ExFil, the paramilitary organization owned by a guy named Cain who used to be the president of Bones MC. Cain did work for the governments of several different countries, including the US, when the CIA didn't or couldn't get involved. I had to hand it to them. They had some grade A shit at their disposal. I might not like depending on anyone other than my club, but my estimation of Bones went up several notches.

"If we're gonna have to wait for a break in the weather, you might want to be ready for a fight." Clutch wiped his face with his arm as he stepped underneath the walls of the hangar. "We got most of them, but I can't be sure we got everyone. And if we missed even one, they'll send reinforcements."

"Get everyone on board," Deke said. "We'll leave in ten minutes."

"You sure the weather will cooperate? I'd prefer the danger I can control to sitting in a tin can that could be blown out of the sky like a fuckin' gnat by this storm."

Deke ignored him and climbed inside the bird without a backward glance.

"You heard the man," I said, turning back to the Humvee. I wanted to get everyone on board as quickly as possible, so we'd be good to go the second Deke was ready to leave.

I went to the back of the Humvee and opened the door. Two of the women flinched and shied away. Dorothy was still asleep where I'd left her. The other two didn't move.

"It's all right. We're getting you guys out of here." Stitches tried to soothe the women, but they didn't look like they were buying it. They glanced at each other before climbing out of the truck and heading toward the hangar when Brick urged them on. Then Brick picked up one of the unconscious women while Deacon got the other. Stitches started to pick up Dorothy, but I shoved my way past him.

"I got her." I didn't want the other man touching her any more than he had to. That was something I was going to have to work out later. Right now, I was going on adrenaline and instinct. And everything inside me was screaming that this girl was mine to save. Mine to protect.

I picked her up, moving us to the back of the vehicle and out the door. It was difficult given I couldn't stand all the way up, but at least there was room to move around.

Once out of the Humvee, I curled myself around Dorothy as best I could to protect her from the sting of the rain, but it didn't matter much. I was soaked. Seconds later she was soaked. She gasped and opened her eyes groggily but didn't say anything.

The Venom rolled out from the hangar. The only reason the big son of a bitch fit in the fucking toy hangar was because the blades folded back behind her. Looked like someone had made some modifications because Venoms didn't typically have landing gear. Bet that voided the warranty good and proper.

By the time we'd all climbed aboard, Deke was rolling through a preflight checklist and talking to someone on the radio. Brick passed out helmets for everyone. Not only were they there for protection, but it would allow us to communicate over the noise.

"Ready for takeoff when you give the word." I didn't think Deke was talking to any of us.

"Ten minutes." I assumed that was the intel guy at Bones. I couldn't remember his name, and didn't much care. "There'll be a small break in the storm. Not a lot, but the wind should be at a more manageable level."

"Roger, Data. Keeping an eye on it here too." Deke was flipping switches and checking a satellite radar of the area and beyond, likely looking at the same information. I ground my teeth and adjusted my hold on Dorothy. She was still passed out, having not opened her eyes since I'd first picked her up.

Something didn't feel right. There was an itch between my shoulder blades that always meant trouble. Granted, the idea of taking off in this weather was a daunting prospect, but I'd been in worse situations.

"Uh, guys?" That was Wylde, the Tzars' intel guy and all-around pain in the ass. But he was our pain in the ass and the man was fucking smart. I expected he'd be monitoring shit, but him interrupting in the middle of an operation meant my instincts had been right. Things were about to go sideways.

"What the fuck are you doing on this frequency?" Deke sounded distracted rather than upset despite his words.

"Backin' y'all up. Also, I hacked into a couple of... uh... things. Y'all got company on the way. So, you don't have ten minutes."

"Fuckin' hell." I slid Dorothy off me and put a restraint harness on her in case Deke had to take off before I could get back to her. All of us readied our weapons, looking around us for the first sign of trouble.

"Two vehicles coming from the south. One from the west. Unsure how many meanies are in each truck, but I'm betting they didn't come light. After that it gets bad."

Deke paused what he was doing for the briefest of moments before glancing back over his shoulder. "Did he just say 'meanies'?"

Brick grunted. "Fuckin' Wylde." I knew how he felt. I wasn't a man to joke where Wylde rarely took anything seriously. "What do you mean it gets bad?"

"I mean, once the third vehicle gets to you, there are five more headed toward you. They're about five minutes behind the ones coming over the hill... now."

That was all we had time for because the first two vehicles did indeed burst over the small rise at that exact moment. Gunfire exploded as they got their bearings. Brick didn't have to give us the order to fire back. It was kill or be killed, and these girls had been through enough.

"How long before the third vehicle is in range?" Deke yelled over the radio, presumably to Wylde.

"Thirty seconds. Get a move on, boys. Time's a' wastin'."

"Fuck." I muttered the expletive as I returned fire. "Ain't sure we can buy ten minutes, Deke."

"Buy me three."

"You got your three," Brick growled. "Not a second more."

"Just keep them off us. I'll get us in the air."

"Will we be any safer in the air, though?" Clutch's muttered question mirrored my own, but I wasn't about to say so. I glanced over my shoulder where Dorothy was slumped in the seat with her harness holding her in place. I was glad she wasn't awake for this, but I was still worried. Why I was anxious over her I had no idea. Probably because she was the first person in my life to not turn their back on me when they found out I'd killed. Stitches made light of it now, but even some of the men in Iron Tzars gave me the side-eye when they found out who I was.

"Here they come!" The second Brick called out the warning, I saw the Jeep jump the hill leading to the hangar. Me and Deacon took the two already on the way while Brick and Clutch focused on the third one.

Bullets pelted all three vehicles. A few hit the helicopter. One of the women screamed, but I heard Stitches behind me trying to talk her down. The helicopter moved, rolling from the hangar.

"Gonna be a bumpy ride," Deke muttered over the comms. "Hang on."

The rotors slid into place from where they'd been folded. Then the engine started humming and whining as Deke prepared to take off.

Gunfire exploded all around us. I took out two men in the first Jeep while Deacon got the tires of the second one. The vehicle swerved, fishtailing before finally flipping and rolling several times before coming to a stop on its top. One man was thrown, landing against a boulder. Blood painted the rock like modern art. I didn't see what happened to anyone else, but the bullets stopped from that direction.

Deacon gave me a nod before we both shifted to the other side of the aircraft. When I turned, Brick was sliding the other door shut. "Did you get 'em all?" Deacon gave Brick an expectant look.

"No. I thought we'd invite 'em to come with us. Be a hell of a party," Brick snapped. The big vice president wasn't usually so snarky, but Deacon was on everyone's shit list. He knew it, too, and didn't rise to the bait. With a sigh, Deacon moved to the one woman Stitches hadn't strapped into her seat and helped strap her in. When he took his seat, he shook his head slightly before turning his attention to his gun, checking it over in case he needed it again.

I glanced at Brick who just scowled. He and Sting were furious with Deacon. It had something to do with Scarlet's sister, Apple. I was sure everyone knew what had happened, but I didn't pay attention to shit like that. If Sting decided Deacon needed killing, I'd do it. It was my job. To kill. Because I might be put in the position to kill anyone, including my own brothers, I kept to myself. I didn't get too close to people and never let anyone close to me. Sure, I was friendly on the surface, but that was as far as it went. If my brothers noticed, they didn't say anything.

"I just wanted to help if it was needed, Brick." Deacon looked like he was as defeated as he sounded. "I meant no disrespect." Brick gave him a withering look and grunted before turning his attention back to the window.

I raised an eyebrow but said nothing as Deke prepared for takeoff. The aircraft shuddered in the fierce wind. One of the women was weeping, obviously terrified.

"*Todas vamos a morir.*"

"No one's dyin'," Clutch snapped more harshly than I thought strictly necessary. "No one!"

Stitches gave him an annoyed look. "Maybe you should absorb that thought your own damn self. No need to terrify the girl further."

Clutch shut his eyes and shook his head slightly. Sweat dripped from his forehead, and he looked ill.

"You OK, bro? You weren't hit, were you?" When I asked the question, Stitches glanced sharply at our road captain, no doubt looking the other man over quickly for injuries.

"No, I wasn't hit," he muttered. "Fuckin' tin can. You can't make a fuckin' tin can fly." Though he groused, I could see Clutch clearly had issues either with flying in general or helicopters in particular.

"Hey," Deke said over the radio. "No disrespecting the bird. She's good in a storm. She'll get us home."

Just as he spoke, the helicopter made a sharp bank to the right. "Ain't as worried about the bird as I am about the pilot takin' us into the fuckin' storm." Clutch was... not in a good way. I was pretty sure he was turning green.

Deke glanced behind him in Clutch's direction. "Don't you fuckin' puke in my ride, man. You mess it up, you clean it up."

"Fuckin' prick." Clutch muttered his response, bracing himself on the bulkhead. "I thought you said three minutes. Has it even been that yet?"

"Yep. Hang on."

"Watch out!" Deacon barked the warning just as more gunfire caught our side of the chopper. Three bullets hit the window, but the glass held. More dinged off the hull as the helicopter banked wildly with what I assumed was a combination of evading fire and the wind.

All of us not strapped in were tossed against each other. I had to catch myself on an overhead bar to keep from dropping my full weight on top of Dorothy. Her eyes fluttered open, and she gave me a vacant look. She obviously wasn't processing anything around her and that was probably a good thing. But it worried me.

"Stitches, I think Dorothy needs help." I managed to hold my weight off her but didn't want to move away from her yet. "Dorothy. Dorothy, honey." I gently smacked her cheek, just hard enough to get her attention.

She blinked up at me. "Morgue..."

"Yeah."

"That's good, Dorothy." Stitches shouldered me out of the way, taking a penlight and looking at her eyes. "You remember Morgue."

"He's killed looootta people." Her voice was slurred but she knew what she was talking about. Lucid, if impaired. "Hopin' he added those fuckin' bastards in that shithole to the tally."

"I think she's all right." Stitches looked in her ears as well as her mouth before looking at her eyes one more time.

The chopper banked sharply again. Dorothy gasped, her eyes snapping open, but she didn't cry out. Instead, her gaze darted around the interior as if looking for the threat.

"Easy, Dorothy. Easy." I put my hand on hers again, giving it a reassuring squeeze. "We're all right. Wind's just a little rough."

"Little?" Clutch snarled. "You call it a little rough? We're on the edge of a fuckin' hurricane!"

"Jesus, Clutch. You're embarrassin' me." Brick rolled his eyes and shook his head. "What the fuck, man?"

"I don't like helicopters, all right? Tin fuckin' cans with a fuckin' beanie on top."

Dorothy gave a little giggle even as her eyes drooped. "I like that description." She frowned. "Never been on a helicopter before."

"You have now, honey." Stitches patted her hand and smiled down at her. "If we're lucky, it'll be a relatively forgettable experience."

"Clearly we're not fuckin' lucky, Stitches."

"Never knew you were such a pussy, Clutch." I couldn't help the jab, especially since Dorothy seemed to be amused. If it took her mind off what had just happened to her, it would be worth Clutch's dignity.

"Ain't no fuckin' pussy." There was a beat of silence. "I like fuckin' pussy, though."

That got a chuckle from Brick and Stitches. Dorothy actually barked out a laugh before she groaned and clutched her side. Even though she was in obvious pain, she still chuckled.

Then, she started crying. Then sobbing.

"Stitches." I gave our doctor a hard look. "Make it stop."

"If you ever figure out how to make a woman stop crying when she has a good Goddamned reason, let me know, will ya?" He sounded put out as hell, like the whole thing irritated him, but he was too amused to commit to being surly. "I'm just glad she's with it enough to realize she's safe now."

"Ain't safe until we land. Safely," Clutch groused. "Fuckin' tin can."

"We're past the outer band," Deke told us. "Still be a bit rough, but smoother."

"How long until we get to Corpus Christi?" Brick demanded of Deacon. And it was a demand more than a question. One Deacon better know if the expression on Brick's face was any indication.

"About three and a half hours. Unless Deke has to land earlier to refuel."

"Should be good," Deke responded immediately. "I think we're runnin' lighter than we expected. The kid's right. Three and a half should be 'bout right."

The flight was considerably less turbulent. Hopefully, Deke would be able to keep us on the outer part of the storm. Because I really didn't want to listen to Clutch ralph all the way to fucking Texas.

When I looked back at Dorothy, she smiled even though tears were still flowing freely. "Texas?"

"Yeah, baby. Texas, then Florida."

"Am I dreaming?" Her smile faltered. "I always wanted to go to Florida. Wanted to move there after school. But I ended up in that horrible place and... Am I still there?"

"No, Dorothy." I tried my best to reassure her but wasn't sure how much I managed. The pain in her voice, the confusion on her face, was almost my undoing. Christ, I needed to get a rein on these feelings. Fast. "I promise you're out of there. And safe."

"You're supposed to be scary. Aren't you." She didn't phrase it like a question.

"Most people think so."

"Have you really killed a lot of people?"

"That frighten you?" I moved slowly to sit next to her, not wanting to startle her or make her feel like I was crowding her.

"To know that you've killed?" When I nodded, she looked thoughtful. Like she was really pondering the question. "It probably should, but it doesn't."

"Good. I don't want you to be scared of me. Just want everyone else to be."

Again, she smiled. "OK, then. I won't be scared of you."

Which, now that I thought about it, might not be a good thing for me. If she wasn't scared of me, I couldn't keep her at arm's length. And she was already seriously under my skin. For no good reason.

Whatever happened in the next few hours, I knew my life would forever be linked with Dorothy's. I wanted her to be mine. I knew this without a doubt. But letting her in meant making myself vulnerable. If you didn't love anyone, you had no one to lose. I'd long ago lost everyone I cared about. All I had were my brothers. I even kept them away as much as I could. Whatever I was feeling for Dorothy wasn't at all comfortable, and I knew I didn't want to become comfortable with it. I wanted to run as far and as fast away from her as I could, even when I knew I never would. This woman was meant to be mine. I just had to be brave enough to take her.

Chapter Three

Dorothy

My head ached. So did every bone in my body. My abdomen felt like someone was twisting my insides in a wringer, and my mouth tasted like a cat had shit in it. And I needed water like I needed air to breathe.

"Ohhhh..." I groaned. I rolled over on my side, expecting the stench to hit me. This place wasn't exactly sanitary, and the only bathroom we had was the bucket in the corner. Not only did the air have a clean, fresh scent, but I wasn't lying on the hard floor.

I opened my eyes and blinked. I was in what looked like a decent-size room. The bed I was in was a queen. The sheets smelled cleaner than anything I'd smelled since my ordeal began... How long *had* it been? Sunlight filtering in from the window created dust motes that glistened like diamonds.

"Where am I?" I wasn't sure who I was talking to, the words coming out on their own before I could censor myself. Was anyone even with me? I tried to convince myself that the last few weeks had been a nightmare, but the way my body ached and my stomach cramped told the truth. I didn't have a whole lot of experience with drugs, but I was willing to bet I was starting withdrawal. It all depended on how long I'd been out and how long it had been since they'd shot me up.

"Evansville, Indiana." The deep voice answering me sounded like it was across the room. "You been out a while. Stitches checked on you to make sure you'd respond but didn't think it was a good idea to wake you as long as you were sleeping peacefully. Sorry 'bout the catheter."

"What?" I tried to sit up, but any movement made my head swim and pound with pain. I groaned.

"Careful," the man said. Then he was at my side, helping me to sit. He put a couple of pillows behind me so I could sit comfortably before moving away. For some reason he sat in the far corner of the room. Trying not to scare me?

I sat there for several minutes just trying to not puke. That's when I realized what he'd been talking about. Between my legs, a rubber tube sprouted, draping over my leg to a bag hanging on the bed frame. Half full of urine.

"Fuuuuck." I picked at the rubber tube, but the man moved back to me and gently removed my hand.

"Be careful. Stitches said you'd hurt yourself if you didn't get it removed properly."

"Who did this? You?" It felt like a violation, though considering what I remembered, maybe it was this was the lesser of the evils.

"No. Stitches. Our doctor." The guy seemed not to say anything not strictly necessary. It was damned frustrating.

I sighed. "Can I have some water?"

Instead of replying, he crossed the room to a small fridge and pulled out a bottle of water, bringing it back to me. He opened the top and held it out. I took it eagerly, gulping down several swallows before my stomach protested.

He gently took the bottle from my hand and set it on the nightstand. "Not too much."

That's when I noticed the tube in the bend of my arm. "What's this?"

"IV."

I gave an exasperated sigh. "Yeah. I know what it is. What I meant was how'd it get there and why?"

"Stitches."

"Right. He's the doctor," I snapped at the guy. I thought I should know who he was but couldn't quite place it. His voice was familiar. Though looking at the guy, I was pretty sure I should be afraid of him, but I wasn't. "You know, words don't cost you anything."

The guy grunted, then scrubbed a hand over his face as if he was weary. "You've been out for almost two days. Stitches started the IV and put in the catheter because he thought it would be better to do it while you slept. He said you'd probably go through some withdrawal and that the longer you could sleep, the less you'd suffer. You also needed to hydrate, so he did it with the IV."

"Yeah," I said, forgetting my ire. "My belly's cramping and I'm nauseous."

"I'll get Stitches."

"Wait!" I reached out and grabbed his wrist. He looked down at my hand before slowly covering it with his own large hand. His skin was warm and as I looked up at him, I could see something in his face. To me, it looked like... awe? But why? I lowered my gaze, tugging my hand, but he didn't let me go. "I'm sorry," I said. "I just wanted to know who you are." I frowned, trying to remember. "I feel like I know you."

He shrugged. "I carried you out."

"Morgue." I said the name absently. His name came to me like a distant memory. "Because you've put more people in the morgue than all of your friends combined." Again, it just came to me. "You got me away and fought off the men following us."

"I helped, yeah."

"You made me feel safe."

Morgue sat up straighter, his chest going out like he was proud of himself. Like making me feel safe was some kind of an accomplishment. "Good. You trust me?"

I thought about it. Did I? The only thing I knew about this guy was he was a killer, but he'd taken care of me when I was in a really bad way. I nodded slowly. "Yeah. I do."

"I'll be back. Stitches needs to look you over and decide what to do next."

He patted my hand before releasing me and standing to leave the room. He opened the door but stopped and turned back to me. "Do you want something? Something other than water to drink? Something to eat?"

I looked down at myself. I was dressed in a man's oversized shirt and nothing else. I cringed, though I figured it was probably Stitches who'd undressed, washed, and redressed me. My hair felt grimy, so he'd only hit the high spots. But there was no denying both men had taken care of my needs as best they could. Hopefully while preserving my dignity, but really, beggars couldn't be choosers. "Well, I'd really like a shower and some clean clothes. Tell whoever lent me his shirt that I appreciate it."

"Mine." Was all he said. OK. We were back to one-word sentences.

"Thank you, Morgue. For everything."

He just grunted, then left. My chest tightened the second the door shut behind him. I wasn't ready to be on my own, and this guy felt safe. Maybe it was how he'd carried me out of hell, how he'd protected me when we were being chased. Or maybe it was because Morgue was a known killer, freakishly huge, and he was fixated on protecting me. Whatever it was, the thought of him leaving and not returning was about to cause a panic attack. I took a breath and closed my eyes, trying to center myself. I was developing an unhealthy attachment to a man I didn't know. I wasn't even trying to fight it that hard.

Once I was alone, I lifted the covers and looked down at myself. My legs were covered in bruises, as were my arms. Pulling up my shirt, I saw that my torso hadn't been spared. I raised my hand to examine my face and head only to wince. My cheek was swollen, and there were at least two knots on my head. I thought I had a split lip but couldn't tell if it was from where someone had hit me or dehydration.

There was a soft knock at the door, and I automatically answered. "Come in." As the door opened, I recognized the man entering. Morgue was right on his heels.

"I remember you too," I said. I thought I trusted both these men, but I still felt at a pretty big disadvantage. I was practically naked, alone with two men I didn't know, and one of them, at least, had seen and touched my naked body while I was unconscious.

He gave me a kind smile. "I'm sorry about the medical stuff, but you and most of the other women were in a pretty bad way."

"You could have taken me to a hospital."

He nodded. "Yeah. But it took us a few hours to get to Texas. Most of you were still unconscious, but no one was in imminent danger. Some of those girls aren't from the States and we thought, since I could treat you, we'd take care of you until you were able to decide for yourselves."

"So, you're saying that if I want to leave now, I can?"

"Absolutely." His response was immediate. When I glanced at Morgue, though, he was frowning at Stitches.

"She's not ready to go yet."

"It's her decision, Morgue." For some reason, Stitches looked amused. I wasn't sure if it was on my account or something Morgue had said.

"She's not ready." He lifted his chin stubbornly, like his word was law and he meant to enforce it. For some odd reason, his attitude was comforting when otherwise I might have really decided to leave. I didn't think I was ready to leave their care. Not yet. I was hurting enough to know I couldn't make it anywhere on my own. Let alone all the way to Kansas.

"He's right," I said softly. "I'm not ready, but when I am, I expect you to let me go." It sounded as stupid as I felt, but I meant every word.

"Absolutely."

"I'll follow you." Morgue looked angry. Not like he was about to kill someone though. More like someone was trying to take away his favorite toy or something. Gun, maybe. His favorite gun.

"Morgue."

"I'll. Follow. Her." Yeah. No compromise there. I probably should have been horrified, but it kind of settled something inside me. I was sure I'd chafe at this strangely possessive man, but for now, I might need him. Just the thought of willingly leaving him made me nauseous. Yeah. I was fucked.

"I won't leave," I said softly. "I don't want to do this alone just now."

"She doesn't want to be alone."

"Jesus, Morgue. What the fuck's wrong with you? I know you can sound like a non-Neanderthal. I've heard you."

I looked from Stitches to Morgue and back. "This is amusing to you?" What was I missing?

Stitches snorted. "Not sure amusing is the word

I'd use, though it is kind of funny listening to him trip all over himself. It's annoying. Not to mention embarrassing as hell. I'm not sure I can be in a club with a man who can't even hold a conversation around a woman." Morgue took a threatening step toward Stitches, clenching his fists and making his biceps threaten the material of his shirt. "See?" Stitches hiked his thumb over his shoulder at Morgue. "Just call him Captain Caveman."

Whoever that was. "Look, I trust you to take care of me and I thought I might like you, but if you don't quit trying to make Morgue look stupid, I may have to stab you in the eye with a spork."

Stitches barked out a laugh and winked at me. "Keep him on a short leash. Man needs to be tamed before he hurts himself. Now. I'm sure you don't want me poking around to fish out this catheter. So what I'm going to do is deflate the balloon holding it in place. After that, all you have to do is pull it out. There'll be some pressure and maybe a little sting, but it shouldn't hurt. I want to keep the IV fluids going and have you drink as much water as you feel comfortable with. You need to use the bathroom before I can leave you alone completely."

"Why? Can't we go on to wherever we're going? Though, I really need to go back to Kansas."

"Right," Stitches said. "I remember. Liberal, Kansas. You got family there?"

"No. But everything I have is there. I was with friends for Spring Break. We were going to Cancún."

"Did you make it there?"

"Yeah. We got there, but she took me to a really poor part of town. It's where Maria lived and where we were staying while we were there. The last thing I remember was going with her to a rave. Whatever happened, happened there because that's where my memory ends."

"You're pretty calm about this whole thing. Do you often get kidnapped?"

Had he slapped me, I wasn't sure Stitches could have surprised me more. If I'd been able, I'd have attacked him. I wanted to strike out at his callousness as much as the implication none of this had affected me or that I wasn't terrified out of my Goddamned mind.

The strength of my emotions must have shown on my face because the next thing I knew, Morgue had Stitches by the throat and slammed up against the wall. "Morgue!" I cried out, stumbling out of bed and toward the two men.

"Dorothy, stop!" Stitches croaked. As he let out his breath to speak, I saw Morgue's grip on his neck tighten. Stitches wasn't struggling. In fact, he'd gone almost limp.

"Morgue! He's not fighting back! Stop!" Morgue looked over his shoulder and gave me a pained look. I wasn't sure if it was because I was denying him a kill or because he wanted to defy me but knew he wouldn't. "Please!" I got tangled up in the damned catheter tube and tripped. I would have hit the ground, but Morgue moved so fast he managed to catch me. I was relieved, but not so much because I hadn't fallen as I was that with Morgue's arms around me, it meant he wasn't busy strangling Stitches to death.

Chapter Four
Morgue

It had been a long time since rage had hit me this hard. The look on Dorothy's face told me Stitches words had really hurt her. There was a combination of disbelief, horror, then unadulterated rage. Also, I was pretty sure she was fighting back tears. So help me God, if she cried because of what Stitches said...

She clung to me, her body erupting in sweat as we stood there. I grunted, lifting her in my arms. The stupid rubber tube was wrapped around one leg and I wasn't sure if it was pulling at her or not, so I sat on the bed with her because the bag was still hanging from the frame.

"Did I hurt you?" I wasn't talking to Stitches. Far as I was concerned, he deserved what he got. Bastard went too far.

"I'm fine," he said, rubbing his neck.

I shot him a look. "Like I give a good Goddamn if you're fuckin' fine." Stitches grinned. Bastard.

"I'm OK, Morgue." Dorothy looked up at me, reaching up to touch my cheek before pulling her hand back just shy of my beard. Like she thought she didn't have the right to touch me. "Really."

"He had no right to say what he did, Dorothy. He's a fuckin' doctor. Everyone works through trauma differently. Ain't his place to say how you deal."

"I know. I think he does too. Probably said that to see your reaction more than mine."

"Keep that one, Morgue." Stitches grinned at me. "You ain't good enough for her, but if you're half as smart as I think you are, you'll convince her you can be so she'll stay."

"You don't know me," Dorothy said, narrowing

her eyes at Stitches. If I'd been in a different frame of mind, or if I hadn't lost my soul years ago, I might have been amused at how cute she looked. Right now, though, I wasn't capable of anything other than baring my teeth at the bastard. "I could be a horrible person. Or not very bright or any number of things. You'd really wish a stranger on your friend like that?"

"Honey." Stitches looked down at her gently. "I've been talking with the women who got out with you. They told me how you hadn't been there as long as the rest of them, but you'd started trying to protect the younger ones the day you got there. One woman said you rarely ate because you gave your scraps to the children. She said none of the rest of them did. They were all just trying to survive. I might not know you, but I know enough about you to know you're a good person."

She took a breath. "Let's table that discussion for another time. Right now, I want this stupid tube gone."

"All right. Let me deflate the bulb, then I'll leave you to it."

Stitches did his thing, then looked at me. "Come on. Let's give her some privacy."

"No."

Stitches scrubbed a hand over his face. "Morgue --"

"No." Dorothy patted my chest but looked up at Stitches. It was like she knew I was getting ready to lay into the doc again and was trying to soothe the beast inside me. "It's all right. He won't look if I tell him not to."

"You trust him?"

"He saved me. I'll trust him unless he gives me a reason not to."

Stitches gave a sigh. "Fine. But I'm sending Iris

and Winter. The women are already taking care of the others we rescued. They wanted to be here with you too, but this brute told them he had it covered."

"Who are Iris and Winter?" Instead of asking Stitches, the bastard, Dorothy looked up at me like my answer determined whether or not she wanted the women there. And I'll be a son of a bitch if my chest didn't puff out. Just a little.

"Iris is our president's old lady. Winter belongs to our enforcer. Winter has a twin sister who is our vice president's old lady."

"Why would they want to be here? To size me up?" Then her eyes widened, and she stood up, snatching her hands from my chest. I didn't like it and a growl escaped before I could stop myself. "President. Enforcer. What kind of place is this?" She took several steps back, stopping only when the rubber catheter between her legs pulled tight where she was basically tethered to the bed. I absolutely could not stand the distance she was putting between us. "I'm not some kind of whore! I know you pulled me out of that hell, but I'm not trading it for another kind of hell!"

I wanted to tell her that, no, this wasn't the same thing, that any women here were here because they wanted to be. That we took care of our own. And that, by God, she wasn't fucking anyone but me! I opened my mouth to say just that, but the words wouldn't come. Not because I didn't believe them, but because, for some stupid reason, I was... tongue-tied around the woman. There was no other way to describe it. I wanted to talk, to make sense and everything, but I didn't seem to be able to.

"Morgue?" Stitches asked. "Say something."

"No," was all that came out. "No."

"'No' you're not saying anything, or 'no' the

women aren't coming here to make Dorothy do something she doesn't want to do?" Stitches sounded like he was about ready to throttle me.

"Yes." Christ. I sucked.

Finally, Stitches took over. "What he means is, the old ladies of our club want to make sure you're OK. That's all. They'll get you anything you need and welcome you into our circle. You do not have to stay if you don't want to, and no one is going to force you to do anything." He paused and Dorothy's gaze shifted to him. Which wouldn't do. So I moved between Stitches and her. "Jesus, Morgue, you're makin' us all look bad. Pull yourself together."

Then I said the strangest thing. "Mine."

"All right, Morgue. That's it." Stitches clasped my arm and tugged me away. "You're coming with me, and the women will take care of her."

"No." I tried to shrug him off, but Stitches had a good hold on my arm.

"Yes," he countered. Only the frightened look on Dorothy's face gave me the strength I needed to allow Stitches to pull me toward the door. "You know she'll love Iris. The women will explain everything to her and help her feel more like herself."

"Not leavin'."

"You want her comfortable. Right?"

I gave Stitches a wary look. I knew he was leading me into a trap. Could even see where he was leading. Still couldn't help myself from answering. "Yes."

"Good. Then we'll leave her to take care of business. The women will bring in some more clothes for her and some electrolyte drink so she's not so parched. She'll take a shower and wash her hair and brush her teeth and all the other shit women do in the bathroom, then they will bring her to the common room for some food. You can meet her there."

I wanted to protest, but knew Stitches was right. The woman had been through hell. The last thing she needed was a damaged, killer biker crowding her space. With a defeated sigh, I nodded and let Stitches lead me to the door. It was no surprise that Iris was already headed our way with an armload of necessities.

"Nyla and Pepper are with the other women. Winter and Serelda had Brick take them to get some more things for everyone. I thought Dorothy might want a few necessities."

"Good," Stitches said, still taking over because, apparently, I'd been reduced to caveman speak. "She's awake and a little jumpy. Could use your delicate touch." He smiled at the other woman.

"Yes," I said, wanting to take an active role in Dorothy's care. I needed everyone to know she was mine and that I could take care of her like she needed, but the truth was, I wasn't sure I could. Oh, I could take care of her. I'd lock her up and never let anyone or anything touch her. But if there was one thing I'd learned from watching the other men find their old ladies, it was that women needed their freedom. I wasn't altogether certain I was capable of giving Dorothy the kind of freedom the other women had.

Iris gave me a quizzical look. "Um, OK. She nervous about where she is?"

"You could say that," Stitches continued, giving me a side-eye.

"Understandable, given where you guys found her. I'll be careful with her." She gave us a gentle smile before knocking on the door and waiting for Dorothy to answer. Stitches tried to tug me after him, but I wanted to wait. I wanted to hear her voice one more time before I left. "Dorothy? My name's Iris. I've got some stuff for you. Clothes. Toiletries. Can I come in to give them to you? I've got some Gatorade and water. You can have either one you want."

After a lengthy pause where I was sure Dorothy would refuse to answer, she finally spoke. "Come in."

Those two little words nearly made me melt. And they weren't even for me. They were for Iris. I wanted to sag in relief.

"Come on, Romeo," Stitches said with a chuckle. "Common room. I'm gettin' you a shot of Jack. Never seen a man who needed it more."

Chapter Five

Dorothy

I'd never been so glad to be alone in my life. Not because I was scared or upset, though I admitted I wasn't as comfortable being here now as I was minutes before, but I could feel the stupid catheter slipping out of me. Fuck my life, anyway.

No. Scratch that. I'd live through a little embarrassment now to be out of the nightmare I'd been in before I woke up in this place.

The second the door shut on Stitches and Morgue, the catheter slipped completely out and plopped to the floor. I nearly groaned in embarrassment as I felt a small trickle of urine running down my leg. Thank God it wasn't much.

I picked up the catheter and bag it was attached to. What the fuck was I supposed to do with that? Thankfully, it wasn't hard to figure out how to empty the bag into the toilet. I threw the rest of it into the trash before finding a cloth to wet and clean myself. Stitches was correct. I wanted a shower. A long, hot shower. I needed to scrub myself clean, though I suspected that might be impossible.

I'd just finished cleaning up when there was a knock at the door. At first, I didn't answer. The shirt I was wearing covered everything, but did I really want to walk around bare-assed in a place with a bunch of strange men? That the line of thought led me to panic.

I took a deep breath just before the knock came again. "Dorothy? My name's Iris. I've got some stuff for you. Clothes. Toiletries. Can I come in? I've got water, and some Gatorade, too."

I tried to tell the other woman she could come in, but my throat was parched. I unlocked the door and opened it a crack.

"Hi, Dorothy." The pretty, petite woman who peered in held an armload of clothes and other things. She didn't look very old, but there was a keen, assessing look in her eyes. She was definitely sizing me up, but not in a creepy way. More like she was trying to figure out the best way to talk to me without frightening me. "I'm Iris. Can I come in?"

I nodded, pulsing the door back enough to unlock the chain and swallowing before I spoke. "Yeah. I'm sorry."

She smiled kindly. "You've got nothing to be sorry for. The men here can be a handful, but they're the best people I know. I brought you some toiletries as well as a couple changes of clothes. Shoes. If there's anything else you need, I'll be happy to get it for you." She set her load on the couch. Then she picked up a moderately sized bag on top of the pile and handed it to me. "Shampoo, conditioner, and shower gel. Also got a new hairbrush and toothbrush and toothpaste. There's also a razor if you need it. Still in the packages." Then she picked up another, smaller bag. "New underwear and feminine products. Do you want me to go while you shower? I can come back if you prefer."

"I, uh. I don't... I don't know."

"Hmm. How about I leave you and come back in an hour. That way you can take your time. I'll bring some burgers and potato salad if you want."

"That sounds delicious." I gave her a tight smile. It really did sound good. I just wasn't sure how much or if I could eat. "I'm a little off-balance. It was bad choices that led me here. I'm afraid to do anything now. Afraid it'll be a bad choice."

"I think all the old ladies here could say the same

thing." She gave me an understanding smile. "You go on and clean up. If you need anything, I'm sure your bodyguard will be just outside. All you have to do is yell for him."

"Bodyguard?" That made my heart speed up. "Am I a prisoner?"

"What? No! Heavens no. I was referring to Morgue. The man hasn't left your side since they got you all here. Morgue isn't one to make attachments easily. In fact, he only interacts with the men of Iron Tzars when he has to. He's decided it's his job to protect you or something. I'm glad, because it's not good for him to be by himself so much."

"Why would he do that?"

She shrugged. "Don't know, honey. But it's obvious to all of us he has. He'll be the best protector you could have."

"He saved me." I have no idea why I said that, but I meant it. I'd felt safe with him from the first time I saw him. I'd pegged him as the most dangerous man in a roomful of dangerous men and put my life in his hands willingly.

"The men here tend to do that. They've saved all of us in one way or another. But we all saved them right back."

I hoped she was right. I felt like I needed saving from my life. Lord knew I could use a fresh start. But was that life here? Or was this just as bad as the other place? I had to admit, though, if the people here were trying to draw me into some kind of sex ring -- like they'd pulled me out of -- they were doing an elaborate set-up. I was scared, but everyone here had been nothing but nice.

Also, Iris was right. Morgue had been with me every time I'd woken up. I'd had vague flashes of waking up frightened or hurting, and Morgue's face was the thing I was able to focus on most. I'd remembered Stitches telling me why Morgue had his name and instead of being horrified or scared, I'd been relieved. Because he was protecting me -- for whatever reason. As far as I was concerned, the more deadly he was the better. It meant no one was getting to me. No one would take me from him. "I believe you. At least, about the first part. I'm not sure I have it in me to save anyone. Not even myself."

"You do." She squeezed my shoulder encouragingly. "I bet you're stronger than you give yourself credit for. You wouldn't have caught Morgue's attention otherwise."

With another sweet smile, Iris left me alone. I thought about what she said while I showered and gave myself a thorough going over. I wasn't sure how long I'd been in that hellhole, but I hadn't bathed the entire time I was there. I knew I looked a fright and was surprised I hadn't fretted about it until now. But my hair was so tangled and matted, I doubted there was any way I'd ever get it brushed out.

I was in the shower for a good thirty minutes. Probably longer. I still didn't feel clean. I doubted all the hot water in the world was going to help, either. My head still wasn't clear. Occasionally, I'd get dizzy, especially with the hot water. But there was no way I was cooling it down. I'd never get clean otherwise.

So, I'd sat on the small bench in the corner of the shower and continued to scrub with more and more soap. Every part of my body. I shaved everything but the hair on my head, which would likely follow later.

By the time I was finished, I'd used half the bottle of shower gel and nearly that much shampoo and conditioner. My skin was red where the water had scalded me. Other than the hopeless mess of my hair, I felt a little better.

The clothes Iris had left for me were wonderful. She'd brought me some sweats, shorts, and three T-shirts, as well as a pair of jeans, socks, and a couple pairs of shoes. One was a pair of motorcycle boots that looked brand-new, the other a pair of canvas shoes with no laces. Looked like they were planning on me staying for the long haul.

I dressed quickly in the sweats and a shirt. I kept the canvas shoes close, but I didn't really plan on going anywhere unless I had to. I was still battered both mentally and physically. And I still had no idea how long I'd been a captive. Besides all that, my belly was really cramping, and I was sweating and shaking and felt like complete shit.

No sooner had I sat down, completely spent after my long shower, then there was a knock at the door.

"It's Iris. Me and Blossom brought food."

I took a breath. Letting strangers in was hard, but these were women, and they were only trying to help. Standing, I crossed to the door and opened it to find the two women with trays laden with more food than I could imagine eating in a week.

"We brought several things so you could choose." The woman I didn't know set her tray down on the coffee table before sticking out her hand to me. "I'm Blossom. Walker is my man. Well" -- she waved her hand in the air dismissively -- "when I claim him. He's a tad ornery. Sometimes I have to kick him in the balls."

I'd shut the door when they entered, but now there was a high-pitched whine and something scratching at the door. I frowned but opened the door again and a dog slunk in, tail between her legs as she looked at me, then hurried to Blossom and lay at the woman's feet.

"Oh, sorry." Blossom gave me an apologetic smile. "Sparkle doesn't like to be away from me. I should have said something, but I honestly don't even think about it anymore. She's always there. I can put her outside if you don't want her in your space."

"No. It's fine. Really." I smiled and squatted down, holding out my hand to the dog. Sparkle crawled over to me, still whining, and tentatively sniffed, then licked my fingers. Then her tail wagged and she moved closer. I rubbed her head and silky ears and the dog looked like she was in heaven.

"Awww, she likes you." Blossom was so genuinely pleased, I couldn't help but smile back at her.

"She's very friendly."

"Sometimes she is. Walker tried to sell her when she was a puppy and she's never forgiven him for it."

"What?" I looked up at her with wide eyes. "Your husband tried to sell your dog?"

"Well, to be fair, he'd already sold the dog before I came along. But Sparkle and me went through shit together and bonded."

"Right," Iris said with a roll of her eyes. "Not Walker's finest moment as I recall."

"He still pays for it when I get miffed at him." Blossom gave Iris a smug smile. "But I love it when he makes it up to me all over again."

Iris snorted. "Yeah. I bet you do." The women giggled. I loved the banter between the two. It was like my roommates at college. That thought made me stiffen. They were like my roommates in college. Which hurt me more than I was willing to admit. Even to myself.

Immediately, Blossom's features grew alarmed. "Dorothy? I'm sorry if we said something to make you uncomfortable. The men here aren't bad. Not by a long shot."

"I'm fine." I was lying through my teeth.

Iris watched me carefully before shaking her head slowly. "I don't think you're fine at all. What do you need? Do you want us to leave?"

"No. Yes. I don't..."

"It's all right," Blossom said. "You don't have to know. Do you want Morgue? Or Stitches?"

"Alone," I gasped. "I want to be..."

"OK. We're leaving," Blossom said, rising slowly. "If you need us or anyone else, just go to the common room. Anyone you see can help you find it, but it's really just at the end of the hall and around the corner."

Sparkle whined and licked at my ankle which, oddly, helped lessen the oppression in the room. I felt like I could breathe easier. I sat back in a nearby chair and Sparkle laid her chin on my knee and looked up at me with a forlorn expression. Like I'd hurt her very last feeling.

I couldn't help it. There was no way I was not accepting the puppy's affection. I sighed, and petted the dog's head, running my hand over and over her head and down her ears once more. She still whined a little, scooting closer and closer to me until, the next thing I knew, she'd climbed up in my lap and laid her head on my arm like a child.

"Well. That's new," Blossom said with a grin. "She's usually only that way with me. And only when Walker does something to piss me off. Most of the time, she's content to lay against me or beside me. When she crawls up in my lap like that, though, she knows I'm feeling it and need some love."

"I didn't mean for her to --"

"No! Not a word. This is what Sparkle does. She's empathetic to the point she has to fix whatever's wrong. The only way she knows how to do that is to love or fight. And there's no one here for her to fight so... Love it is."

"She's helping." I tried to smile but was sure it was a little strained. "Things... were bad where the others found me. I have no idea how long I was there or exactly what they did to me, but I was lured there. By people I thought were my friends."

"It's all right." Iris looked as reassuring as she could given the circumstances. "When someone you've trusted betrays you, it makes it hard to trust strangers."

Shock pulsed through me as I looked at her. "You really do know. Don't you?" There was something in her expression that said she did. It wasn't hurt so much as fury.

"Before Sting brought me here, me and my sister, Jerrica, were in a group home." She gave me a tight smile. "An orphanage. Our parents were dead. We had no family except each other. When I turned sixteen, I got an emergency emancipation, hoping to give myself a couple of years so I could adopt Jerrica out of the home. A little over a year later, I took Jerrica to a Christmas party at a club in Lake Worth, Florida, called Black Reign MC. They always have a huge community Christmas party and make sure all the group homes in the area are there every day they can be until Christmas. Lasts pretty much the whole month of December." She smiled like she was remembering a particularly special moment before continuing.

"Anyway, the night of the actual Christmas party, when I took Jerrica back, they said they adopted her out. That they didn't tell me or her it was going to happen so there was less drama or something. When I came back the next day -- I was there every day, no matter what -- they told me she was gone. They said she'd been adopted. In reality, they'd sold her to a trafficking ring."

"Oh, my God! No!"

"Seems hard to believe, I know. I ran back to the only place I could think of to help. Black Reign. Sting was there because he needed to talk to Warlock. Warlock is Sting's father. He'd resigned as Iron Tzars' president and Black Reign wanted him at their club." She waved her hand dismissively. "Not important. Sting was there when I came running to the compound. He heard my tale and offered to help. El Diablo, the president of Black Reign, accepted the offer, and they rescued Jerrica and all the other children who'd been sold from the group home."

"What you're saying is, the men here are good guys."

"Yes, but mostly I'm saying I understand why you'd find it hard to trust people you don't know. Especially after being betrayed by people you did know."

"Thanks, Iris." I swallowed a lump in my throat. "Everyone here has been nothing but good to me." I tried to chuckle. "Except for the catheter. Stitches did it because I needed it, I suppose. Doesn't mean I have to like it."

Sparkles whined, bringing my attention back to her. "Sparkles, if you weren't already spoken for, I'd keep you with me." She licked at my hand before jumping out of my lap and going back to Blossom to sit at her feet. I smiled. "Well, she might be a great therapy dog, but she is firmly yours."

Blossom smiled at Sparkles. "She is. But she'll stay with you if you need her to."

"No. I think I'm fine. You can sit down and eat with me if you want." I looked at all the food. There were hamburgers, hotdogs, baked beans, coleslaw, and all kinds of fruit and vegetables to eat with dressing. Then there was sweet tea, milk, beer, and water and electrolyte drink packs for the bottled water. "Wow. I hope you didn't expect me to eat all this."

Blossom grinned. "I expect you to eat what you want. If there are leftovers, I'm sure someone around here will eat them. They always scavenge. Anything not already growing penicillin is fair game." She wrinkled her nose. "Kinda gross, actually."

That got us all to giggling. I felt lighter, but still not entirely comfortable. And I didn't really know what to do to make it better.

"Everything all right in there?"

Blossom and Iris grinned at each other. Iris answered before I could say anything. "I don't think Dorothy's feeling well."

There was a brief pause, then the doorknob jiggled. "Open up."

"Is that Morgue?"

Iris winked at me. "Sure is. Now, don't you worry, honey. Just sit back and let things happen."

Blossom nodded. "It's the easiest way."

"Let what happen?"

"I'm coming in." Morgue's voice was harsh, angry sounding. I had the chance to suck in a breath when the lock on the knob snapped and Morgue charged inside. "What happened?" His gaze found me the second he was in the room. "How'd you hurt yourself?"

Blossom stood. "Will you be OK with Morgue?"

I blinked up at her, not sure what to think or feel. "I think so? Maybe?"

"Of course, she'll be OK with me," Morgue snapped. His focus turned to me and he looked me up and down. "What's wrong? What hurts?"

"What?" Was this really happening right now?

"She said you're not feeling well. What's wrong?" There was no doubt his questions were actually demands. His eyes were wide, and he shoved a hand through his hair. "Well?"

"I, uh, well, I think I might be having some withdrawals?" I looked up at the women who were waiting to make sure I was good with them leaving me with Morgue. "I didn't tell anyone."

"Iris, get Stitches. Tell him Dorothy needs stuff."

"Stuff," Iris said, covering a grin by clearing her throat. "Got it."

Blossom gave a little finger wave. "You kids have fun." Then she and Iris left. Sparkle gave me a "wuff" and licked my ankle again before moving in the direction of the door. She paused and looked at Morgue on her way, baring her teeth and growling once before continuing after Blossom.

"Well," I said, not sure what was supposed to happen next. "That was… interesting."

"Sit down," Morgue bossed. "Where does it hurt?"

"I think I'm fine. But my stomach hurts. Just kind of, I don't know, cramps. Little nauseous."

"You're trembling." He knelt in front of me where I sat, taking my hands in his. "You're sweating, too." Morgue got me a bottle of water and opened it for me. "Drink this."

"You're kind of bossy."

Morgue just grunted. He took out his phone and

sent off a text before focusing back on me. "How long have you been feeling like this?"

"Since I woke up. I get dizzy sometimes, but I figured it was the drugs still in my system."

"Probably." He stared at his phone, frowning. "Fuckin' bastard. Answer my fuckin' text." He tapped at his phone again, looking up at me occasionally, like it was important for him to keep an eye on me. He swore again as he looked at the screen. Then he punched something else before putting the phone to his ear. Making a call. "Where the fuck are you, Stitches?" I heard the other man speaking from the phone, but Morgue cut him off. "Never mind. Get to my room. Now. Dorothy's sick."

"Quit your bitchin', you big bastard." Stitches entered the room, rolling his eyes as he moved to my side, crouching down and placing a duffel bag on the floor. "I can't teleport from the common room."

"You were taking too long."

"It took me less than two minutes."

Morgue shrugged. "Felt longer."

Stitches pulled out a bag of fluids and a bunch of other things. "You realize you're going into withdrawal. Right? Do you know how long you were there?"

"Uh, not really. What day is it?"

"The twenty-third."

I blinked. "Wow. I thought it was longer than that. Way longer. We got there on the fifteenth." I tried to grin, playing it off like a bad joke. "Worst Spring Break ever."

Morgue shot Stitches a sharp look. "Right." He crouched down so he wasn't looming over me.

"Yeah." I looked back and forth between them. "My roommates talked me into going to Cancún.

Didn't I tell you that?"

"Yeah, but I didn't realize you thought it was still March or April."

Dread crept through me, and chill bumps broke out over my arms. "So it's the twenty-third... of May?"

Stitches winced and Morgue reached out, resting his hand on my knee, palm up. Obviously wanting me to take his hand. So I did. "No, baby." Morgue closed his hand around mine and took a breath. "It's June."

I felt like I'd been kicked in the gut. I shook my head. "That's not possible." My voice was barely above a whisper.

"OK." Stitches took out his phone and sent off a text, all business now. "Couple things need to happen now. First, I'm getting you some stronger antibiotics than what I've already given you. Then I'm setting you up a different IV with some vitamins and electrolytes. Should help keep you hydrated." He shook his head slightly. "I can't give you anything for the pain other than some anti-inflammatories. I'll keep open the possibility of starting you on a five-day course of Suboxone, but I don't want to use it unless I have to. I don't like treating narcotic withdrawal with another narcotic."

I was getting overwhelmed. OK, I was past overwhelmed and edging toward a full-blown panic attack. I'd been in that horrible place for more than two months! I could almost deal with the time frame. What I couldn't deal with was the haze over my memory. "I don't... I can't..." My breathing started coming in small gasps and my head, which had been aching before, now thumped mercilessly. "What did they do to me?"

"Don't think about it right now," Stitches said gently. "Let's just work through the main concerns one thing at a time."

I met Morgue's gaze and held it. The man looked fiercer than I'd ever seen him. The look on his face should have frightened me because he looked like he was ready to do murder, which he'd already admitted he was capable of. Instead, it grounded me. He wasn't angry at me. He was angry on my behalf. At least I hoped he was.

"Morgue." Stitches squeezed his shoulder. The other man flinched but allowed the contact. "Why don't you go get the women? She'd probably feel more comfortable without so much testosterone in the room."

"No." His denial was gruff, and his gaze didn't leave mine. His hold on my hand tightened fractionally, like he was afraid I'd pull away. "I'm stayin'."

"For Christ's sake, Morgue. She's been traumatized enough. They all have."

"I'm staying."

Stitches shook his head, but I spoke before he could. "I don't want Morgue to leave." I have no idea why I said it, but the second I did, I knew it was true. I felt safe when Morgue was with me. Probably because he carried me out of hell and protected me.

"All right, then." Stitches scrubbed a hand over his face. "I'm still going to send Iris back. I'll be back with some more meds."

I nodded, the numbness over my emotions gone like ripping off a Band-Aid. The pain was sharp and intense, and I wanted to scream but didn't dare. The last thing I wanted to do was show more weakness in front of these people. They probably already thought I was stupid. Hell, *I* thought I was stupid.

When Stitches shut the door behind him, Morgue

moved to sit beside me on the couch, then pulled me onto his lap and into his arms. Those big, muscular arms closed around me securely, but loosely and I just melted against him. The second I did that, all the grief, pain, and anger came flooding out of me.

I buried my face in his neck and screamed. Sweat erupted over my skin and I shook uncontrollably, the enormity of what I'd been handed too much to handle. I sobbed and bunched my fists in his shirt, clinging like he was my lifeline on a cliff. In a way, I suppose he was. Since I'd first become aware of what was happening, Morgue had been the one I'd looked to, to make sure everything was as good as it was going to get. I trusted him. I liked that he was protective of me, that he'd claimed me in a way. Maybe not for the long haul, but for now. And that was good enough for me. Because, despite knowing I'd been sold out, despite all the pain I'd gone through because I'd trusted the wrong people, something inside me needed this man. A man I didn't know, but a man who'd gotten me out of hell. If I couldn't trust Morgue, there was no one in the world I *could* trust.

Chapter Six
Morgue

It felt like I was going to erupt in a fit of rage. I wanted -- needed -- to slaughter every motherfucker who'd done this to her. Sure, me and my brothers had killed everyone we knew of in the place Dorothy had been kept, but I now included her roommates in my hate. I didn't like having to kill women, but I knew I'd relish these deaths.

And Goddamnit, I wanted her to see me as a man who could and absolutely would protect her! My entire adult life, I'd been Morgue. The man who killed, and killed willingly. It had never bothered me before. Now? I wanted Dorothy to see me as more. A man willing to do what was necessary, but...

"Why?" she sobbed out against my neck. "Why did this happen?"

"Gonna take care of you," I said. I wasn't sure why, because, a nurturer I was not. I was a killer. I could avenge her, could rain down death and destruction to her enemies, but I'd never been the overly demonstrative type. "Then I'm gonna kill everyone responsible for this."

She cried for a long while, trembling in my arms. I tightened my hold on her, doing the only thing I could think of to make her feel more secure. Her crying lessened but didn't stop. So, I held her tighter.

Finally, she calmed down to the occasional sniffle. She didn't pull away from me or indicate in any way she wanted me to let her go, so I didn't.

"You know," she said, her voice shaky. "It could have been an innocent accident. They might not have known this was going to happen."

"Know soon. Got Wylde lookin' into it."

"Wylde?" She didn't move and sounded like she was exhausted. Probably was, given the release of emotion she'd just spent.

"Intel officer. Does shit with computers."

"Oh. OK."

We were a pair. Now she'd devolved to one-word sentences too. Nothing more needed to be said anyway. I held her and she let me. That was all either of us needed for the moment.

All too soon, there was a knock at the door signaling Stitches and possibly the women too. I growled in frustration. Though I knew she needed them, I wasn't ready to give up this peace yet. Selfish, but she seemed content and I knew I fucking was. So, when she stiffened, I barked out, "Go away!"

There was a slight pause. "Morgue, it's Iris. I'm coming in."

"Go away!"

"It's all right," Dorothy whispered. "You can let them in."

"Don't want to."

Dorothy didn't say anything else and didn't move to get out of my arms. When the door opened, I groaned in protest.

"Relax there, big guy," Iris said, entering slowly with Blossom. Sparkle didn't have the same hesitation. She trotted straight over to us and licked at Dorothy's ankle, whining as she did so.

"What can we do, Dorothy?" Blossom ignored me altogether. "We can't take the pain away, but we can give you something else to think about for a while."

Sparkle whined and pawed at the seat next to me and Dorothy before slinking up and turning around in the corner, so her muzzle lay against Dorothy's legs.

She could stick her tongue out and lick Dorothy's ankle.

Dorothy leaned forward to reach for the dog. Sparkle whined when Dorothy stroked her back a couple of times but didn't move other than to lick Dorothy's ankle again. Seemed that was how the dog was going to comfort Dorothy.

"I think Sparkle is gonna do much better than us." Blossom gave Dorothy a gentle smile. "You let Sparkle stay with you until she wants to come back to me."

"But won't she want you?"

Blossom shrugged. "Sparkle knows when someone needs her, and that's where she goes. If someone is hurting, she's right there trying to give any comfort she can. If you need her to play, she'll play. If you want to snuggle? She's your dog. If you just need someone to watch over you, she's that too. Trust me when I tell you that Sparkle will not leave until she's sure you no longer need her."

Dorothy nodded slowly before settling back against the crook of my neck. "OK."

"Good. Now." Iris brought out a phone and laid it on the coffee table in front of us. "That phone has all our numbers programmed in. You know me and Blossom, but there's also Bellarose, Odette, Danica, Nyla, Piper, Winter, Serelda, and Scarlet. You can call or text any of us at any time and we'll come to you. No questions asked. All we want is for you to feel safe." She gave me a glance before continuing. "I'll leave it up to Morgue to add his number and anyone else's he thinks you need."

"Thank you. I'm sorry to be such a bother." She sniffled and I thought I might lose my mind if she started crying again. Never thought a woman's tears would affect me like this, but they made me feel helpless and like I wasn't caring for her like she needed.

"You're not a bother, honey. We've all been through something. Maybe not as horrific as what you've gone through, though some of us have, and we know that the biggest part of healing is finding a place where you feel safe. Physically safe as well as safe to be yourself. The men here gave us that. As the female population grew and the men started finding women they wanted to keep, we took up the banner and let me tell you, it's much easier for a woman to feel safe when surrounded by women who have their back. That's us."

"The men have our backs and that puts us all solidly in the center," Blossom continued. "They make an impenetrable wall around us."

Dorothy lifted her head and looked at the women, studying them before nodding her head slowly. "I like that."

Iris let out a breath and smiled. "We've got you, honey. All of us."

Stitches knocked on the doorframe even though the door was open. "Got some stuff," he said. "Startin' with the bug juice."

Dorothy wrinkled her nose delicately. "Bug juice? Didn't know alcohol was a cure for… uh, stuff."

"It's not." Stitches gave her a grin. "Bug juice is also Doctor slang for antibiotics. Though, sometimes I recommend alcohol. One shot of Jack never hurt anyone." Not strictly the truth, but I saw what Stitches was trying to do.

"I didn't know there was such a thing as doctor slang." Dorothy lay passively again, her hands curled into fists and still bunched in my T-shirt.

"Sure is. Ask any doctor."

As if on cue, Eagle, our club's medic, knocked on the doorframe just like Stitches had. "Someone order some bug juice?"

"Yep. Give it to Iris. She'll help me."

"Sure thing. Want me to shut the door?"

"Please," Iris answered. "Thanks, Eagle."

"Sure thing." Eagle nodded at Dorothy and gave her a small but friendly smile. "Welcome to the family, lil' bit. We got your back."

"Thank you." Dorothy's answer was soft, but she managed to eke out a smile for Eagle. I didn't like her giving her smiles to the other man, but at least she wasn't crying anymore.

The next couple of hours was filled with Stitches infusing antibiotics and fluids. Stitches found non-narcotic solutions instead of narcotics. Not as immediate, but it took the edge off. The IV fluids seemed to help her more than anything.

"Aren't you gonna ask me embarrassing questions?" Dorothy spoke so softly I wasn't sure Stitches heard her. Wasn't sure I would have if her mouth hadn't been so close to my ear.

"No, honey." Stitches gave her a smile. "At this point, what happened doesn't matter from a medical standpoint. I gave you a broad-spectrum antibiotic. It'll kill most infections. If you start hurting or have unusual smells or discharge, we'll reevaluate. At some point, you may want to talk to someone. When you get there, I'll find someone you can be comfortable with."

"That's just it. It's all a haze. I didn't even know how long I'd been there. I think that, maybe for the first few weeks, they kept me so doped up I had no hope of being aware of everything. I've never even smoked a joint or had more than a wine cooler to drink."

"Yeah. I could see that. You're lucky you didn't overdose."

She tilted her head, seeming to think about what he said. "If I remembered what they did to me, I might well have wished they had given me an overdose. So maybe me not remembering is a good thing."

Stitches shrugged. "Not a bad way to look at it, honey. Just keep the offer in mind. I'm a doctor so I look after your medical as well as your mental needs. Ain't no therapist, but I know several good ones."

"Thank you. For everything."

"You're welcome. I'm glad you're here with us, Dorothy." Then Stitches glanced at me. "Take care of her, Morgue."

I grunted.

Finally, when everyone was gone and it was me, Dorothy, and Sparkles -- the dog hadn't moved other than to lick Dorothy's ankle occasionally -- she lifted her head and looked up at me. She took several deep breaths. It was obvious she was trying to get her thoughts together because she opened her mouth a couple of times like she was going to speak but didn't.

"Just rest. You need something, you tell me."

"Am I in your home?"

I nodded. "Yeah. If you're uncomfortable with that, we can move to a different room."

She pushed away slightly then, looking at me on more of an even level. "We? I mean, you don't have to go with me. I just don't want to take over your space."

A disgruntled growl escaped before I could censor it. "Stayin' with you."

"Are you sure? I mean, I'll sleep on the couch, so you'll still have your bed, but I don't want to be all up in your shit."

"You won't be. And you'll sleep in the bed. Not the couch."

She fidgeted a little, picking at my shirt. "I don't..." She swallowed, two tears overflowing before she swiped at them with her hand. "I don't want to be alone."

I let go of a breath I hadn't realized I'd been holding. I wasn't sure I was capable of leaving her alone while she slept, even if it was my bedroom and I'd be right outside the room. What if she had a nightmare? I wanted to be there to soothe her immediately. "You won't be. I'll be with you."

She was quiet for a time, not moving, but she didn't close her eyes. I'd give my right nut to know what she was thinking. Was she scared? Of me?

"Thank you, Morgue. I'm sure I'm cramping your style, but you'll never know how much I appreciate you letting me melt down like this."

I grunted. It was becoming my go-to response. Why? Because I couldn't seem to get my bearings around the woman! She was battered and broken. Had been drugged out of her mind. There was no hoping she hadn't been raped or sexually abused in God knew how many ways in the time she'd been there. She'd simply been a captive too long. I was surprised she wasn't beaten worse than she was. My guess was they kept her so doped she couldn't do much more than lie there and take it.

What I wanted to tell her was that she never had to worry about anything ever again, least of all being hurt by anyone. She was mine and I protected what was mine. Somehow, though, I doubted that would help matters any. She might feel comfortable with me now, but laying claim to her would change the dynamic.

I wasn't sure how long we stayed like that. I think I might have dozed off at one point. Dorothy did too. It wasn't until Stitches came back to change out her fluids that either of us stirred.

"Just swapping out bags," he informed us softly. "How you feelin', kiddo?"

"Better," she replied. "My head doesn't hurt as much, but my belly is still in knots."

"Yeah. Give it a few more hours. The fluids will help."

She managed another small smile. "I believe you. I think they've helped already."

"That and the ibuprofen. Once this goes in, I can remove the IV if you like. Or I can disconnect the bag and leave it in case you need more tomorrow. Would save you a stick."

She nodded. "I think that will be best. If it's not too much trouble."

"Honey, nothing is too much trouble to make you comfortable and to help you heal. But I'd feel better leaving it in, to be honest."

It took another half hour for the bag to finish. Stitches taped up her IV site so she didn't get it caught on anything, then left us. Dorothy didn't move, but I knew she probably needed to use the bathroom.

When I shifted on the couch, she whimpered and clung tighter. Sparkle lifted her head and whined slightly, licking at Dorothy's ankle again.

"Ain't goin' nowhere. Just thought I'd carry you to the bathroom. Do your business and we'll go to bed."

"You promise you won't leave?" She looked up at me with pleading eyes and my heart melted.

"No fuckin' way I'll ever leave you, Dorothy. I'm yours as long as you want me." Again, her eyes filled with tears, and I panicked. "I mean, I'm not gonna force myself on you or anything. I just mean I'll protect you. Always."

She wrapped her arms around my neck and the fucking tears started again. She pressed herself close to me as she cried. Every single tear felt like a dagger to my heart. Dorothy was clinging to me, so I held her tighter. If she didn't want me, surely she'd push me away. There was no way to let her go when she was so distressed.

"Do you promise?"

"Yes. I won't leave. I told you."

"No." She shook her head but didn't pull away. "That you're mine. As long as I want you."

I narrowed my gaze on her. "I fuckin' promise, Dorothy. I Goddamn fuckin' promise."

Chapter Seven

Dorothy
Three weeks later...

"Morgue?" For the first time in weeks, I woke up alone. Even when he woke up before me, Morgue was always at my side. Just like he'd promised, he didn't leave me. "Morgue!"

"In here, honey." His muffled voice came from the bathroom where I now heard the shower running. My heart rate slowed, and relief flooded through me. He'd left the bathroom door open. I should have known. He was never more than a room away, and never with anything between. Not even a closed door unless he told me why, which was always the bathroom. Anything else, he did with me in the room.

I was lucky. So very fucking lucky to have Morgue with me. If I needed a reminder of that fact, all I had to do was spend time with the other women they'd pulled out of that place. All of them were scared of their shadows. When I looked into their eyes, I saw women who'd given up hope. They'd accept their fates, whatever they were, and wouldn't lift a finger to defend themselves. They all needed protectors like Morgue, but I wasn't giving him up. Not for the other women. Not for anyone.

I climbed out of bed and padded to the bathroom, leaning against the door. The shower walls were clear but fogged with condensation from the hot water. I'd watched Morgue shower every day, and I never got tired of looking at his naked body.

He was thickly muscled. Tall and powerful. Not for the first time, I wanted the right to trace all those muscles with my hands and lips. I never thought I'd feel this way about a man after my captivity, and I probably never would about anyone else. But Morgue? Yeah. I really wanted him to be mine. I wanted to be his. He never gave me any indication he was sexually attracted to me, and I think that hurt more than I was willing to admit.

"Are you watching me again?" Morgue didn't pause as he washed his hair and beard. Ducking under the spray, he rinsed away the shampoo, scrubbing his hands over his head and face.

"Do you mind?"

"You know I don't."

I took a tentative step toward the shower before I could stop myself. Taking the collar of his T-shirt I wore in my fingers, I tucked my thumb into the material and brought it to my nose. I always stole his shirt after he took it off at the end of the day. It smelled like him, and I loved having the scent surrounding me. Not that it mattered much what I wore. By the time we woke up each morning, his scent was on anything I wore. It often made me wonder if my skin would smell like his if we both slept naked. Fanciful thinking, I knew, but the more time I spent with Morgue, the more I realized that, even if we'd met under different circumstances and I didn't see him as anything but who he was and not my hero, I'd still want him with every fiber of my being.

He rarely smiled, was surly as a goat, and as antisocial as anyone I'd ever met. But he was loyal and honorable. He kept his word to me, no matter what he had to do. I was helpless to guard my heart from him, even if I tried.

"Would you mind if I joined you?" I have no idea where I found the courage to ask that question, but I wanted permission to be in there with him.

Morgue faced me, shaking his head and slinging

water in all directions. He scrubbed a hand over his face, wiping water out of his eyes. He placed his other palm on the clear shower wall, giving me his front. There was no disguising his interest. His cock stood at attention in the nest of dark curls at his groin.

"You're always welcome anywhere I am, Dorothy. I think you know that." He'd started using more than one- and two-word sentences a couple weeks ago, a sure sign he was more at ease with me. His words flowed more effortlessly now, the dark timbre of his voice sending thrills through me when I never thought I'd feel this way again. Hell, had I ever been this aroused?

I held my ground, unyielding to the intensity of his stare. "I'm not afraid of you, you know." I didn't make a move toward the shower but didn't take my gaze from Morgue. All that muscled, tattooed skin was mesmerizing and utterly captivating.

"If you were, I doubt I'd be in your bed every night, holding you while you slept."

"I think, technically, it's your bed."

His response was instant and insistent. "It's as much your bed as it is mine." If he looked amused or anything other than deadly serious, I didn't see it. "Either way, you sleep in my arms every fuckin' night when no one else ever has, woman. You have me."

I took that as the invitation it was, peeling off my shirt and panties, then climbing into the shower with him. The water hit me in a gentle spray, tickling my skin. Morgue kept his gaze on me the entire time. He studied me like I studied him. Hungrily.

"Nothing happens you don't want to happen, Dorothy. You can stop at any time."

"What makes you think I'd want to stop?"

He shrugged. "Sometimes, things that seem

comfortable at the time don't stay that way. I'm a big man. The last thing I want is to accidentally frighten you."

Desire won out over caution. I had the feeling it always would with Morgue. I closed the distance between us until our bodies nearly collided with each breath we took. "Of all the people in the world, Morgue, you are the one person who could never frighten me."

I placed my palms on his chest and slid them upward until I wrapped my arms around his neck, pressing my body against his. Morgue's hands rested on my hips.

"If you don't want me to kiss you, I suggest you step away."

Instead of stepping back, I smiled up at him. "I got in here hoping to do more than kiss you."

"You sure?" He tightened his grip on my hips, still holding me securely even as he tried to give me an out.

"Do you really want me to move away from you, or is it that you feel like you have to give me the choice?"

"I do have to give you the choice. It's always your choice."

"Then I choose you. But only if you want me back."

He chuckled then, a soft laugh I hoped would always and only be for me. It was one of the few times I'd heard him express amusement. Pulling me close so that his hard cock mashed into my belly, he grinned at me. "Pretty sure this means I want you back, baby. I'll take whatever you want to give me and be thankful I was your choice."

"Good." I breathed the word as I pulled myself

up to kiss him.

He was gentle as he kissed me, coaxing when I wasn't sure I needed convincing. I loved that he was gentle at first, then, as I responded with more and more fervor, he became more aggressive. Nothing too overt, but he left no doubt how much he truly wanted me. He moved one hand from my hip to gently cup a breast, teasing my nipple into a hardened peak. The sensation ignited a fire within me that threatened to consume me.

With the water sluicing over us, Morgue continued to tease and tug at that nipple while he kissed me with wicked flicks of his tongue.

He groaned against my mouth as I kissed him back. He was so hard, and it felt so good to have his arms around me. His heart pounded against my chest as if we shared the same heartbeat. For now, Morgue was the only thing keeping me from despair, who made me feel anything other than terror after those terrible weeks before he'd rescued me.

He ran his fingers gently through my hair as I held onto him tightly, a reminder of how careful he'd been when he'd detangled my hair in those first few days I'd been fully awake and alert. I remember telling him to just hack it off and he'd grunted his displeasure. Then he'd taken the next two hours and patiently, carefully, worked through the matted mess until he could run the comb through it without even a hint of a snag.

The feel of his wet, hair-roughened skin against me was even better than I could have imagined. After everything that had happened to me, I thought I would feel at least a sliver of panic, but all I felt was safe. I thought the passion I was feeling now as he expertly played with my body should scare me, but I embraced it eagerly, needing this. Needing Morgue.

I slid my hands down his torso, tracing the lines of his tattoos, feeling each ripple of muscle under my fingertips. He let out a low grunt into my mouth as I playfully bit his bottom lip.

"Woman," he growled. "That little dance is gonna get you in trouble."

"What dance?" I asked with mock innocence. "This one?" I nipped him again.

His arms went around me like steel bands as he held me close. "Damned straight, that fuckin' dance. Dreamt about this moment so many fuckin' times. When I held you. When I watched you interact with my club. Every fuckin' time you look at me like I'm your lifeline. 'Cause you're damned sure mine."

I whimpered, need riding me even harder at his rough confession. "Me too. I wish I'd been brave enough to tell you before."

"You're the bravest person I know, Dorothy. You're dealing with your life as it is now. Maybe slowly, but you're dealing. Some of the others aren't. You know that because you've done everything you can to help those women. Makes me so fuckin' proud."

His lips found mine again, and he kissed me with more fervor this time. As he slid his tongue into my mouth, he bunched his fist in my hair. It wasn't hard, but it definitely had a bite to it. Strangely, instead of being a trigger to some buried memory, all I felt was a spike of heat.

I moaned into his mouth and curled my arms around him, so my nails raked from his shoulders down his back. He jerked at the slight pain, a deep growl building in his throat.

"Woman… fuck!"

He bent his knees, adjusting his hold around me,

then lifted so that I had to wrap my legs around his waist as he walked us to the bench at the back wall of the shower.

Planting a knee on the bench, he laid me on my back. It was a cramped fit, but when he shoved my legs to my shoulders, he had enough room to kneel and bury his face in my pussy.

"Morgue! Oh, God! Yes!" My cries were loud, echoing off the walls.

Morgue's rough beard scraped against my inner thighs as he growled against the soft, wet flesh between my legs. His hot breath fanned the sensitive folds of my pussy, and he didn't tease anymore as he lapped at me. One hand held my knee pinned against my chest, his fingers digging into my skin, while the other squeezed my breast roughly, pinching my nipple between thumb and forefinger.

I cried out again, arching into his touch as he sucked on me like he was starved for me. He got up, leaving my clit exposed to the spray of water. Wrapping one arm around my back, Morgue moved me again. This time, he sat on the bench with me straddling his hips, our bodies pressed together as he ground his cock against my belly. He was big, and I shuddered in anticipation.

Morgue paused. "You good, baby?"

"Yes," I breathed. "But I'm not sure how much longer I can wait." I pulled back to cup his bearded face in my hands. "I can't stress enough how much I really want this, Morgue. Want you."

"Yes," he growled. "Want you." Yeah, he was devolving again, but I loved it. I could actually feel him trembling as much as I was. "Fuckin' need you, woman."

His other hand cupped my face, holding me still

for his kisses. He took possession of my mouth again. This time it was truly a possession. He wasn't holding back, and it fueled that fire he'd so effortlessly created.

Our tongues danced wildly together, and I moved against him, stroking his cock with my belly. As I opened my eyes, I watched the water droplets roll down his body, his muscles flexing and pulsing under his slick skin as he held onto me like I was all that mattered in his world.

I'd never been kissed like this. Hard, demanding, then soft and caressing. It left me breathless and needy for more of him.

I latched onto his neck, nibbling at the skin just above his shoulder. When he pulled back, it was to position his cock between my legs, aiming for my pussy.

"Ready?" His gruff question made me all the hotter, wanting him. Needing him to fuck me like he meant to keep me.

"More than. Please, Morgue! I need this so much!" I was on the verge of crying, I was so turned on. I'd never really understood the phrase "hurts so good" until now. There was pain when he pulled my hair, but I fed off it. There was the pain of unfulfilled desire when he didn't immediately fill me with his cock. And, when I came, I knew the intensity would be a shock to my innocent system, but I knew I'd embrace it. I'd never been with a man before Spring Break, and I didn't remember anything that happened during my captivity so, as far as I was concerned, this was my first time.

Slowly, carefully, watching my every expression, Morgue slid inside me. There was a sharp pinch I hadn't expected to feel, and I gasped. Sex wasn't supposed to hurt once your hymen was broken. Right?

"Dorothy, talk to me." He'd stopped, and I wasn't sure I wanted him to continue just yet.

"It's nothing."

"It's not nothing. Talk." He reached up and turned off the water. He shook his head, sending water droplets flying again before scrubbing one hand over his face to clear his vision of the water. When he finished, he gave me a hard stare.

"There's... there was a... something. A sharp pain. But it's easing off already."

As if testing me, Morgue slid farther inside me. Not much, just enough to test my reaction. When I continued to meet his steady gaze, he slid in farther until he was seated as far as he could go. Instead of immediately pulling out, however, Morgue pulled back, spreading my legs as wide as they would go. When he pulled back, he did so slowly with his gaze fixed on my pussy. His brow furrowed, his features tightening. "There's blood."

"What?" I raised up on my elbows to look between us. Sure enough, a thin trail of blood smeared over his cock.

"You hurt? Or is it time for your period?"

I looked up at him, confused. "It pinched a little at first, but it doesn't hurt at all now. And maybe? I don't know!"

He shook his head once, then slid back inside carefully. When he pulled back out, there was still a small amount of blood, but it was less than before. So, he did it again. With each movement, every time my pussy stretched to accommodate his girth and my clit got friction, my body threatened to combust. There was no more blood. The thought that maybe I'd managed to squeak through that place without being raped wanted to form in my mind and with it a relief so sharp and stark it would have sent me into a sea of tears and snot. But I wasn't going to focus on that just now. Because, if that wasn't the case, my devastation would be just as hard as the relief.

"Sweet God," I moaned, arching my back. My tits thrust upward. "That feels so fucking good!"

Morgue grunted. Instead of continuing, however, he pulled me into his arms and picked me up, still impaling me on his cock. I gave a little squeal, but he ignored me as he stepped out of the shower. We were both soaking wet.

He snagged a towel before setting me on the vanity and placing the towel around my shoulders. With brisk movements, he dried me, then gave his upper body a little going over before he put his hands on either side of my hips and gave me a fierce look. He was still inside me. "Now. Tell me. How much did I hurt you?"

"It was only a small pain, Morgue. Honest. There, then gone. The pleasure is so much more than the pain, and it's not even fading now. It's completely gone. There's a little bit of a burn where you're stretching me, but it only adds to how good this feels." I could feel tears gathering in my eyes. "Please don't stop. Please. I need to know what..." I closed my eyes as two tears coursed down my cheeks. "I need to know what comes next."

"Fuck." He scrubbed a hand over his face. This time, instead of getting rid of water, I got the feeling he was trying like hell to figure out what to do. "You swear, Dorothy? I mean, really fuckin' swear?"

I couldn't help but grin. "Yeah. I really fuckin' do."

There were several beats of silence, then Morgue barked out a laugh. Then chuckled. Then outright guffawed. Tears streamed from his eyes in his mirth, but his cock was still hard as stone inside me. "You are a rare treasure, my little Dorothy. I am proud to call you mine."

I thought he might fuck me then, take me and push us both over the edge. Instead, he wrapped his arms around me again and carried me back into the bedroom and moved us both on to the bed. I thought he would settle himself over my naked body, however, Morgue rolled us gently so that I was on top of him with his cock still inside me.

"Now. You want this, you do the work," he said. "I'm not gonna hurt you because I'm so fuckin' horny I can't control my fuckin' self." He swept his hands up and down my hips and thighs in a soothing yet tantalizing caress. When I didn't immediately move, he urged me up and down, and I understood what he wanted me to do. I braced my hands on his chest and started riding him.

It took me a minute to get the right angle, but the second I did and my clit scraped over his skin with every motion, my movements became more assertive. I gasped as I moved, my hips snapping forward and backward as I rode him. Morgue's breathing was heavy and deep, the occasional grunt broke free, but he was otherwise silent, watching me intently.

I threw my head back and screamed. The peak I'd known was on the horizon crested but was shy of what I thought it would be. I was missing something I had no idea how to express. Or maybe this was all there was?

"Dorothy?" Morgue hadn't taken his pleasure. I think he was too busy making sure I was OK to let himself go.

"I'm sorry." It was all I could think of to say.

"Thank you for this." I started to climb off him, but Morgue grasped my hips, stilling me.

"What's wrong? You have to talk to me."

I smiled at him. "We both seem to devolve to one- or two-word sentences on occasion. I'm not sure the conversation would be all that informative."

"You need something else." It wasn't a question. "Tell me."

I shrugged helplessly, doing my best to fight off tears. "I don't know! There seemed like there was going to be more than... I don't know. It just went away."

"Did you have sex before you left for Cancún?"

I shook my head. "No."

"So, you were a virgin."

"Yes."

Very slowly, probably so he didn't frighten me, and I had time to stop him if it triggered me, Morgue rolled us until he settled his weight on top of me. The change was immediate. I gasped as he rocked his hips from side to side to position himself comfortably.

"You tell me if it's too much or you don't like me pinning you down. Yes?"

"I promise."

Morgue started to move then. His hips moving in a slow, sensual rhythm. Every motion sent more and more friction over my clit. My breath hitched as I climbed that elusive peak once more. When he leaned down to kiss me, I thrust my hips back at him. It was instinctual on my part. It just felt good.

"That's it, baby. I'm gonna take care of you." His words were between kisses and against my lips in a breathy whisper. "I'll always take care of you."

I dug my heels into his ass, urging him on like spurring a horse. Morgue complied. This time, his breathing was as ragged as mine and I knew he would never lead me wrong in sex. He'd always find the best way to our mutual satisfaction. That was the moment I realized that I'd never want another man. Never. Only Morgue. And I didn't even know his name.

The epiphany shook my concentration just enough for me to fall over that peak I'd been heading toward before I had the chance to fully appreciate it. It was like starting up that first major hill on a roller coaster and immediately dozing off. Then, the second you wake, you're starting over the hill, looking straight down at the track but unable to see the bottom. It was fucking terrifying. And I screamed in ecstasy.

Chapter Eight
Morgue

I hadn't left Dorothy alone for more than a very few minutes since she'd come here three weeks before. I'd promised her I wouldn't, and I hadn't. But the discussion I was getting ready to have was something I needed to do without her around to hear the conversation. Thankfully, Dorothy still had Sparkle on loan, and Blossom and Iris brought all the old ladies by to visit with her. I'd told her where I'd be and I had my phone so she could call or text if she needed me, then gone to Wylde's office. I'd called Stitches to meet us.

"Tell me you found those bitches," I started the second I walked into Wylde's office. Needless to say, the other man was less than impressed.

"Nice to see you too, Morgue. Welcome to my office. Where I shoot pushy bastards on sight."

"Wylde, just give it to him. Don't go pissing off the man in the club with the most confirmed kills. M'k?" Sting sounded amused but resigned. I knew the feeling. Most days, I wanted to pinch off Wylde's head. The man was a pain in the ass. He was also brilliant with a computer.

Wylde sighed, like Sting had just taken his favorite toy. "Fine. But if you ask me, Morgue needs to lighten up a bit. All that aggression will give you gas."

"Do you have something or not? I left Dorothy to be here."

"Pussy whipped already, are you?"

I glared at the other man. "Don't make me go to Danica. If anyone's pussy whipped, it's you."

"Right. But Dani and me have been an item for a couple years now. I have a right to be pussy whipped. You've only been with your woman a couple of weeks.

That's way too soon to be pussy whipped."

"Christ," I bit out. "Imma kill the sumbitch."

"Wylde, now really ain't the time. Do you have something or not?" Stitches gave me a worried look. Yeah, he knew I was only mostly kidding. Sort of.

"Bottom line, your girl's roommates sold her out. It was a carefully planned and premeditated event intending to sell her into sexual slavery." He shook his head slightly and frowned. "OK, so they didn't really know what would happen to her, just that she had admitted to being a virgin and they were selling her to someone who would pay top dollar for virgin women."

There was silence in the room before I turned and punched a hole in the wall with a war bellow. Someone was going to die. And I absolutely would not feel the least bit of remorse, no matter who I had to kill.

"Yo, man! Calm ya tits!" Wylde stood, moving to stand between me and the wall. "Got wires running through there, and I don't want to have to fix shit you broke."

"Wylde, what do you have linking Dorothy's roommates to her disappearance?" Sting was trying to bring the focus back to the business at hand to redirect me, but it was damned hard. All I could think about was getting vengeance when I needed to be cold and calculating. It was a position I hadn't found myself in for a very long time.

Wylde snorted. "I got all the things. Texts and phone calls from the burner phones they used, emails from dummy accounts, I even managed to find some footage of them at the rave they took her to. That wasn't easy, by the way. I had to piece together video footage from cell phones of people who were there in the same time frame. It's the main reason it took me this long to have anything." He shrugged. "Might have broken a few international treaties or some shit, but I got it. I also happened to find some really good blackmail footage on four or five prominent people in the US and abroad. You know. If you're interested. Might come in useful." Then he continued. "Here's the really diabolical part. No one knows Dorothy's missing. Well. Except her roommates."

Sting cocked his head. "Come again?"

"Yeah. They got Dorothy set up with online classes the rest of the year and through the summer. Been loggin' into her account regularly to make them think she's still present and accounted for. Doin' a couple things in her classes so no one gets suspicious. Spoiler alert -- she's now failing everything now when she was an honor student before."

"So, you're telling me, there is no one looking for this girl?" Stitches traded a look with Sting. "No one. No family. No friends."

Wylde shook his head. "Nope. Kid's mother died from an apparent accidental overdose when Dorothy was sixteen. There's no biological father listed on her birth certificate. No other living family that I could find. Any friends she had were at school, and they all think she's taking a mental health break from in-person classes. Text came from her phone and every Goddamned thing."

"So, by the time anyone realizes she's missing, her roommates can swear they saw her last week," Stitches commented dryly. "No one will be able to say for sure she disappeared during Spring Break and those bitches will be in the clear."

"Uh, correction," Wylde said with a raised finger in the air and a cocky grin on his face. "Those bitches *think* they'll be in the clear." He plopped back down in his chair and pointed to the bank of computer monitors on his desk. And the wall. And the couple on the ceiling. For when he leaned back in his chair? Crazy fucker. "I got videographic evidence as well as all the supporting shit to back it up. *If* you choose to take them to court, once I set up a realistic chain of discovery, they'll be goin' away for a long fuckin' time."

"Ain't goin' to fuckin' court," I growled. "You point me in the right direction and I'm going to disappear them."

"Agreed," Sting said without hesitation. "But we're takin' it a step further. I want the people she was sold to and everyone in between."

"I'll bring her roommates to the barn," I said. "I'll get everything out of 'em they know."

"Not sure you're the right one for the job this time, Morgue," Roman said as he entered the office, phone in hand. I glanced at Sting who shook his phone at me with a raised eyebrow. Wasn't long until every officer in the club was crowding in Wylde's office.

"Right one or not, it's a job I'm takin'. She's my woman. It's my right to do what I do best."

"You sure about that?" Brick asked calmly. "What if she never sees you the same way again? You willin' to risk that when there are men here perfectly capable of takin' this on?"

"I am." I didn't hesitate with my answer.

"Morgue." Stitches put a hand on my shoulder. "You're her safe place right now. Are you sure, really sure about this?"

Damned bastard knew exactly what to say to make me hesitate. "I'll talk to her."

"She know she's your woman?" Brick exchanged a look with Sting. I knew what they were thinking.

"She does. But she doesn't know all the details yet. I'll discuss this with her, but I will be going after the people who hurt her, and Dorothy will be good with it."

Wylde grinned. "You're so cute, Morgue." He glanced at Sting. "Ain't he? Gonna just lay down the law to the little woman, are you?"

"For Christ's sake, Wylde." Brick smacked the back of his head. "Stop pokin' the fuckin' bear."

"Hey, I'm just sayin'. Morgue ain't around women all that much. I doubt he realizes that, sometimes, you end up doin' what they want you to do whether it's what you intended to do or not."

Roman grinned. "Hmm... I got nothin', Brick. Wylde ain't wrong there."

Stitches gave me a long, hard look. Then shook his head. "You know, I'm gonna agree with Morgue on this one. Dorothy will be fine. Only thing she'll have a problem with is the separation."

"Which won't be more than twenty-four hours at most," I said.

"You seem pretty sure, Stitches." Wylde narrowed his eyes. "You got eyes on Morgue's girl?"

I couldn't help it. Everything inside me rebelled at the very thought my brother might want my woman. I never claimed anyone or anything, other than my bike and my guns, as my own. Even my bike was negotiable. But if Stitches had eyes on Dorothy, I'd kill the motherfucker.

"No one's killin' no one," Stitches said, raising his hands. "I don't have eyes for your girl, Morgue." Had I said that out loud? "Yeah, man. You did."

I took a breath, trying to calm myself. "Sorry." I shook my head to clear it. "Not really."

Wylde chuckled. "Yeah, I think we all know

where you stand with Dorothy. Now. What I'm interested in is why Stitches thinks I'm wrong. When it comes to women, I'm the man." He tapped his temple. "I know how they think."

"Don't listen to him, boys." The feminine voice came from outside the office. She didn't enter but kept talking. "He knows jack about women. Which is why he has me."

"Dani," Wylde groaned. "You're gonna ruin my reputation." The damned man just grinned.

"No, I won't. Everyone knows better. Besides, you only said that 'cause you saw me pass by."

"You ain't wrong, darlin'."

"Look," Stitches continued. "Dorothy trusts Morgue. She trusts him to keep her safe and it all started with her knowing he was a straight up killer. I have no doubt that she'll be OK with anything he has to do here. Her only hang-up will be him leaving her for an extended period of time."

"Told you. Less than twenty-four hours. If the women stay with her and Blossom lets her keep Sparkle for a while longer, she'll make it." I wasn't budging on this. While we all would do what was necessary, most of the men here would hesitate to hurt women, even if they needed it. "I'll do what needs doin', and I won't let them off easy."

"They won't be," Sting said, straightening where he'd been leaning against the wall. "Are they still at school for the summer, Wylde?"

"Yep. Think they had to be, so it looks like Dorothy is logging in from school. That's the agreement I found admissions has for her. She's at school but taking the classes online. The reason is that until she graduates, campus housing is her home. Before that, she had an apartment in Liberty, which is two and a half hours from the University of Kansas. Wasn't a practical commute and she couldn't afford an apartment in a college town when she had grants and scholarships to pay for her housing. So all her roomies took some summer classes to keep the ruse going."

"Good. You've got two weeks to move. That gives you time to plan and time to reevaluate if you don't have a viable plan in place before then."

"Won't need that long."

"I know." Sting gave me a steady look. "But you're gonna plan this to the letter with Wylde, then submit it to me. Once I'm satisfied it's a sound plan, I'll give you the go ahead. Also, I'll want to talk with Dorothy before you leave."

I lifted my chin. "You think I won't tell her the truth?" It was a challenge -- one I knew better than to issue to Sting.

Instantly, Sting's mien hardened. "No, as a matter of fact, I don't. I think you'll do anything you have to for this kill, even lie to your woman. Which I will not allow," he snapped. "Tzars is for life, Morgue. She has to be good with this." He stabbed a finger in my direction. "So you will tell her everything and give her a choice. One she's gonna have to go over with me and Iris."

I grumbled but didn't argue. Mainly because I knew it wouldn't do any good. "Fine. I'll go talk with her now. I'll get Wylde my plan by tonight. I'd like to leave tomorrow."

"For the love of God," Brick muttered. "Good luck, Sting. Let me know if you need someone to knock his big ass out." Brick left with a wave and a shake of his head. "Stubborn bastard," he muttered on the way out.

Chapter Nine

Dorothy

I didn't like this situation one bit. "I don't want you to go," I said, clinging to Morgue as we lay in the bed together. He'd come back from his meeting with Sting and the rest of his club and had immediately taken me to bed. Which I'd loved. What I hadn't loved was when he told me he was leaving.

"I have to, baby. One day. Just one day. Maybe less."

"But can't someone else do it?"

He was silent for a long moment before he answered, which told me he was at least thinking about it. I had the feeling, though, he wouldn't change his mind. "Someone could. But it's my job. Not only is this my job in the club, but it's never been so important to me to *do* my job. This is for vengeance." He tunneled his fingers through my hair and pulled my head back so he could look at me. "Does it bother you that I'm gonna kill those women? And possibly torture them before they die?"

I shook my head, knowing this would be his concern. "I couldn't care less what you do to them, Morgue. If they did this to me, they've likely victimized other girls who didn't have someone looking out for them. I'm betting my lack of permanent ties is an important reason they chose me. What bothers me is for you to do it." I reached up to stroke his cheek. "If something goes wrong, if you get caught? I can't live with that, Morgue. I can't live without *you*."

"You won't have to, honey. This is what I do. What Iron Tzars does. Wylde makes sure all the bases are covered. Sting has the final say in the plan, and he won't let me go if the risk isn't acceptable."

"How do you define acceptable?" I demanded. "Because as far as I'm concerned, if the risk isn't zero I don't want you to have any part of it."

He gave me a gentle, almost tender smile, stroking my chin with his thumb. "Don't think anyone's ever worried about me before. Let me do what I'm trained to do, honey. Ain't no amateur. Besides, the guys in Tzars ain't gonna let anything happen to me. We look out for each other."

"I still don't like it." I knew Morgue liked to give me anything I wanted.

He grinned again. "You're trying to manipulate me with that adorable pout, but it won't work. Do you trust me?"

"You know I do. With all my heart."

"Then trust me to take care of this. All I'm doing is getting them and bringing them back here. I'm not spending any more time away from you than I have to. But this has to be done. And I have to be the one to do it."

I rolled over so I lay on top of him. "Fine. but I want it known this is under protest."

He grinned. "Noted. I'll make it up to you."

"When?" I demanded.

"Right now." He tightened his fist in my hair and brought me down for a kiss. My heart was pounding as my pussy found his cock. I held us there for a moment, wondering if Morgue would take the lead. I should have known he would. Our bodies aligned perfectly, and he thrust upward, my pussy engulfing his entire length in one smooth glide.

I sank my nails into his shoulders and let out a low moan as he continued to kiss me, his tongue dancing with mine playfully. The taste of him was intoxicating. Whisky and mint should have been an odd combination, but it was perfect. And it only made me want him more. He ran his hands up and down my back, and I shivered with pleasure. I gasped when he nipped my lower lip and pulled back just enough to say, "Please make sure you come back to me, Morgue. I really mean it when I say I don't think I can live without you in my life."

"Nothing could keep me from coming back to you, Dorothy. Nothing. I'll be careful. More careful than I ever have before because, for the first time in my life, I've got someone to come back for. So yeah. I will not be taking any unnecessary risks."

"You promise." It was a demand more than a question.

"I do, honey. I promise with all my heart."

I sighed as Morgue kissed me again and I started riding him. His arms came around me and I settled into his embrace once again. I tunneled both of my hands through his messy hair and hung on as he urged me to move faster.

I never wanted to let go. Morgue was my rock. My anchor. In the short time I'd known him, he'd become the most important person in my world. I remember thinking this the first time we'd made love, but knowing he was leaving soon made the feeling all the more acute.

Suddenly, he growled and rolled us over, so he was on top of me. Still holding onto my hip firmly with one hand while using the other to slide up toward my breast. With a needy moan, I raised my hips to meet Morgue's thrusts, my back arching with each deep plunge of his cock inside me. The friction felt so good, and I wanted him deeper, but I could feel him swelling inside me and knew he was close. I didn't try to stop him. Instead, I gripped his shoulders tighter and let him set the pace.

His hot breath on my neck sent shivers down my spine as he pumped into me, his grunts of pleasure mixing with my moans of lust. I loved the way he claimed me like this. Like he never wanted the use of anyone's body but mine. Like he was as lost in me as I was in him. It excited me more than I could ever express.

He pulled out of the kiss and nipped at my earlobe, suckling it lightly before growling low in his throat as he came, filling me up with his seed. His orgasm triggered my own, and I cried out in release. His hips jerked against mine once more before he collapsed on top of me, our bodies gliding together in a sweaty embrace.

Morgue panted heavily as if trying to catch his breath while I played with the hair at the base of his neck and held him close. He smelled amazing -- like leather and sweat and masculinity that intoxicated me beyond reason.

"Morgue?" My voice was a little hoarse, but I loved the sound. Like my man had been making me scream in ecstasy. Oh, wait...

"Yeah, baby?"

"There's two things I want to know before you leave."

"Anything, baby." He was still catching his breath and sucking on my neck, his beard a shade ticklish.

"Um, well, first of all, do you still mean it when you told me you were mine as long as I wanted you?"

He pulled back, frowning at me. "Yeah. I meant it." He looked like he was sensing a trap, but also like he was pissed I'd make him repeat his promise.

"I only ask because I never want you to not be

mine. And I want to never not be yours either."

His frown deepened. "Neither of those things will happen. I'm yours. You're mine. End of story." Yeah, that was kind of cute. Not that I'd ever tell him.

"Well, you see, if that's the case, I mean, do you believe in getting married and stuff?"

"Yeah, Dorothy," he said. His frown not showing any signs of letting up. "I do. And you will absolutely marry me. You get me? Also, you need to know being my old lady makes you part of Iron Tzars. You ain't a member, but you're a permanent part of this club. We don't divorce. I keep you happy, you stay with me. Forever. Not up for negotiation. No one leaves the Tzars."

I had to hold back a grin and barely managed. I didn't figure this was a good time for him to feel like I was laughing at him. I wasn't. It was just so cute the way he thought I'd balk and not want to stay with him.

"Yeah. I get you. And if you're good to me -- which I know you will be -- then I won't want to leave." I bit my lip then. "Which brings me to the second question."

He lifted his chin. "What."

"Well, I'd kind of like to know, um, your name?"

There was silence. Morgue's lips parted, then he closed them again. With a sigh, he lay back on top of me and kissed me again. This time it was slow and languid. He didn't stop for a long time. When he did, he put his lips by my ear and whispered, "My name's Max," he said. "Max Grimwood."

Then Max "Morgue" Grimwood, the most deadly man in a club full of deadly men, gave me the most wonderful, lust-filled ride of my life.

Several times.

And I loved every blistering second of it!

Chapter Ten

Morgue

The plan was simple. It was Friday night. The women I was looking for always went to the same club. Wylde confirmed they were still on for the evening by hacking into their phones and monitoring their phone calls and texts. There were three of them. I had Stitches, Deacon, Blaze, and Ace with me to remove the women from the club, and Clutch driving the cage to take us out of the city.

Once again, Deke from Bones was waiting in a secluded area an hour outside of Lawrence, Kansas. He'd fly us back to a point just outside of Evansville, to an abandoned farm that just happened to be owned by someone who didn't exist but which had advanced security protecting it from prying eyes. And the occasional hunter. Sting and the rest of the officers would meet us there. We had a barn with a basement specially made for situations like this. Because these women were going to die. Just not right away, because we needed more information from them.

The club the women frequented was small but loud. It worked in our favor in that no one would care if they screamed. Hell, everyone was screaming. The bass thumped, and partiers jumped around in what I assumed was dancing. The only thing I really cared about was getting the three women out of here without anyone noticing anything was wrong. Wylde was on the cameras and all of us who'd gone inside the club had covered up our tattoos just in case. Nothing was foolproof.

It was kind of fitting. They'd brought Dorothy to a club and let her be drugged and kidnapped. So, when I watched as Deacon slipped a Molly in the drink of the woman he was flirting with, I couldn't help but smirk. What was that movie line? Life's a bitch, and her stripper name is Karma. Yeah. I didn't feel sorry for the bitch. None of them.

The same scene was playing out with Ace and Blaze. All three men plied the women with booze and Ecstasy. One of them started feeling the effects pretty quickly, though it seemed to make her more compliant and happy rather than energetic. She was easily gotten to the cage. The other two took an hour before they were flying so high they were agreeable to anything. Once we were all in the cage, Clutch took off for the rendezvous point with Deke.

"I can make you feel *realmente bueno, el cariño*." This was the woman with the residence on the outskirts of Cancún. Since we'd been in the SUV, she'd slipped from English to Spanish and back several times. She was currently all over Deacon.

"Sure you could." Deacon looked disgusted, his nose wrinkling as if smelling something decidedly unpleasant. "How about you take a nice nap." He tried to unwrap her hands from around his neck but, honestly, the woman was like an octopus.

"You taking us to *tu casa*?"

Ace snorted. "You could say that."

The woman with Ace had her head in his lap. She was nosing his crotch, but Ace had managed to keep his fly zipped. He stroked her hair absently with an amused grin on his face. I was pretty sure she thought she was giving him a blow job. Stitches looked to be in a similar situation while Blaze's charge was out cold.

"All right, that's enough." Stitches shoved the woman with her head in his lap upright. She screeched but said nothing intelligible. Stitches zip-tied her hands behind her back and her legs at the ankles. When she continued to scream, he shoved a rag in her mouth and used a strip of duct tape to cover it. "This is fuckin' ridiculous," he snapped. "Tie and gag the other two." Stitches was the ranking club officer on this trip, but he rarely gave orders. Not like this.

"Thank Christ," Deacon said.

"Oh! *Papá* likes a little kink." I thought her name was Maria, but I didn't really care. What I did care about was the fact this woman was the ringleader, according to Wylde. And Wylde would never have made that kind of accusation unless he knew for sure.

"Yeah, Papa likes kink," Deacon muttered. "Just not with skanky cunts like you."

"You bastard!" Maria tried to strike out at Deacon, but not only was her aim shit, but Deacon snagged her arm and pulled it behind her back at a painful angle. "Ow! You're hurting me!"

"Oh, you know what you did to deserve this. You're gonna hurt a lot worse before you die." Apparently Ace had reached the end of his rope.

"What? I-I don't know what you're talking about."

"Right." Ace snorted. "'Course you don't."

He snagged a zip tie from his vest and looped it around her wrists, pulling it tight. Maria screamed again. "I said you're hurting me! What the fuck?"

"Hurting you? What about the woman you hurt? You think she begged?" I asked the question in a deadly growl. "You think they listened? Maybe if you beg long enough and loud enough, I'll listen. Or not." The smile I gave her through the mirror was pure evil. "Either way, we're gettin' ready to find out."

At that, Maria's eyes grew wide. She opened her mouth to scream, but Ace stuffed a rag inside her mouth and taped it shut. Now, the two women who were awake looked terrified. But not terrified enough.

Everything went as planned. Deke got us back to Evansville where Brick waited with the SUV ready to take us to the barn. Wylde covered our tracks so we weren't busted for an unlogged flight path.

We got the women into the barn and into the basement where they were tied with their hands above their heads. They were still gagged. The third one was slowly waking up but was still out of it.

"Give it a couple more hours and she should be awake," Stitches said, nodding to the groggy one. "Then we can begin."

I nodded, walking to Maria and reaching for the tape over her mouth. With one hard yank, I ripped the tape off.

Maria screamed, though the sound was muffled because of the cloth still in her mouth. Once she'd quieted down, I pulled out the cloth.

"Now," I said with a small smile. It wasn't a kind smile. "You've got a little bit to think about what you want to tell me."

"Not tellin' you shit, *cabrón!*"

"Yes. You will. But we'll get to that in a bit. You can stand there and invent all the lies you can to convince me to believe, or you can just come clean and tell me everything I want to know."

"Right," she sneered. "Because I'm gonna do what you want." She spat in my direction. "Go to hell!"

"I might see you there someday. Won't deny it. But you'll be in hell long before I will."

The other woman looked from me to Maria and back with wide, terrified eyes. Tears tracked from her eyes and sweat beaded her brow. She was getting the idea things were about to get serious.

"*¡Cuando salgamos de aquí te voy a matar, bastardo!*"
Maria screamed. Her fury would have been funny if *I*
hadn't been so furious. These women were responsible
for everything Dorothy went through before I found
her. Now, it only fueled my anger.

In a move as sudden as it was spontaneous, I
backhanded Maria hard enough to knock her out. She
went limp, her body hanging from her wrists. I never
thought hitting a woman would ever give me
satisfaction, but there was no denying I liked knowing
I caused pain to Maria. I knew she'd sold Dorothy to
men who would have hurt her, raped, and beaten all
those women if we hadn't rescued them.

It was about two more hours before Stitches was
confident the worst of the effects of the Ecstasy had
worn off all three women. Maria, the mouthy one, was
yelling and threatening while the other two were still
gagged. I'd singled out Maria because she was the one
who'd pushed them to take Dorothy. The others had
gone along with it but wouldn't have on their own.
Didn't mean they got to live. Just meant they had a
better chance of a quick death. Because I was about to
scare the Holy Spirit out of them.

Sting and Brick, as well as all the officers of Iron
Tzars, were witness to what was about to happen.

"You think you're gonna fuck me, *cabrón*? You're
all going to die!" She sneered at me. "Go ahead. If you
can get your pencil dick to work." She gave me a
maniacal smile and bit out, "I like it rough."

"I'm sure you do," I said. "But you're not gettin'
fucked. First, we don't do that. Even if you deserve a
little tit for tat."

"I didn't do nothing to that *perra!*"

"Sure you did." I pulled my knife from the
sheath strapped to my thigh, examining the blade. It

was a wicked, serrated knife with a thick hilt. "I already know this because we have your phone and text records. Even from the burner phones you thought were untraceable." I leaned in to whisper to her. "They weren't." Wow. I hope Wylde was proud of himself. I'd been hanging around him so much I even sounded like him. But, hey. It was better than the one- and two-word sentences I'd been reduced to when I'd first met Dorothy. The mere thought of her put me in the frame of mind I needed to complete this task. "Torturing women isn't really my thing. But I'm making an exception. Just for you. So, here's your choices. You can continue to be a little cunt and last for days or even weeks, or you can tell me what I want to know and go quickly without suffering." I shrugged. "Make your decision."

She barked out a laugh. "You don't scare me."

"Really?" I grinned.

"Yeah. Crazy American. You think we're stupid? You're not gonna do anything to us."

I lunged forward and stabbed Maria in the shoulder with my knife, burying it to the hilt. She screamed over and over with every breath. Then I pulled it out slowly, and she sobbed out her pain.

"Now," I said, picking up a cloth laying on a hay bale and cleaning my blade. "You understand I mean business. Yes?"

"What do you want! Why are you doing this! ¡No hice nada!"

"Oh, but you did do something, Maria. You sold out my woman. Your roommate. I want to know who picked Dorothy up at that rave. And I want to know who your contacts are."

"I don't know anything!" When I stabbed her other shoulder, she screamed again. This time, hysterically, thrashing and trying to kick out even though her ankles were still zip-tied.

"Oh, I think you do. His name is Enrique. Right?" Maria's eyes got wide, and she nodded before she could stop herself. "See? That wasn't so hard. Was it?"

"He'll kill me," she sobbed. "I can't tell you anything!"

"Oh, honey," I said with mock sympathy. "Didn't you realize? You're dead already. There's no getting past this." She whimpered as tears flowed freely down her face. Sweat trickled from her forehead to mingle with her tears. The coppery stench of her blood permeated the basement and overrode the musty, damp smell I normally associated with this place.

"Look," she pleaded. "It was a one-time thing. He needed a virgin, and he overheard Dorothy talking about how she wanted to pop her cherry while she was in school. He came to us."

"Ah, see? That's gonna cost you."

"What? No! No!"

I picked up an axe leaning against the wall and rested it on my shoulder. "I'll give you this one chance to change your statement. After this, you get no free passes. Now. Did Enrique really contact you?"

"Yes! I swear!"

I tsked and shook my head. "I'm sorry I have to do this, Maria." I tried to sound like I truly regretted what I was about to do. The reality was, I could never regret hurting this woman. She was evil to the core. All three of them were, but especially this Maria.

I swung the axe down, severing most of her toes. Maria cried and screamed. She did it some more when Stitches heated a flat blade with a propane torch and cauterized the wounds on her feet and her shoulders. This was when she passed out the first time. Nothing a bucket full of water to the face wouldn't fix.

"You still with me, Maria?" I snapped my fingers in front of her face while she screamed. Gone were her threats and lies. All she could do was scream.

After that, the other two were more forthcoming. When we were all satisfied I'd gotten all I could out of those two, Roman shot them in the back of the head. That's when Maria finally gave up her other contacts. Some of them Wylde had already tracked down through her own contacts. Not all, but enough to keep her honest.

I kept at her until Wylde said she'd told us about every single contact he'd linked with her. It wasn't enough to shut this ring down, or even fully evaluate it, but it was enough for a start.

"What a fuckin' mess," I grumbled.

"Gettin' squeamish in your old age?" Wylde clapped me on the back as he grinned at Maria. "Almost done. Just gotta finish that one off." The woman whimpered, but, honestly, she wasn't in much shape to know what was happening.

"Nope. I just prefer the clean, quick kills. Though I like knowing I got a little vengeance for Dorothy."

Stitches approached us. He'd been making sure Maria wasn't in danger of dying before we were ready. Now he scrubbed his hands on a damp cloth. "Morgue's got himself a fine woman, Wylde."

"I've seen her with the other women you guys rescued. She's patient and kind. Not to mention the old ladies love her."

"That reminds me. Where's Walker?" I looked around the big room for the hunter. "I need a favor."

As if he'd been waiting for me to mention his

name, the man in question tapped me on the shoulder.
I turned around and gave him an annoyed look.

"You could have said something."

He shrugged. "Whacha need?"

"A dog."

Walker nodded. "Blossom said Sparkle's been a
big help to Dorothy. You wantin' one of her own?"

"Yeah."

Walker got a big grin on his face. "I've got just
the dog."

* * *

Dorothy

Morgue was true to his word. He made it back in
just under twenty-four hours. He took a shower and
insisted I come with him where he fucked me against
the shower wall. Then, after we'd dried off and
stumbled to bed, he fucked me again. We dozed for a
while, then I woke him with a blow job and he'd
fucked me again. Then it was time for the serious stuff.

"What happened to them?" I asked. I didn't
really care, but I think I was testing him. Seeing if he'd
tell me or if he'd lie.

He sighed. "Do you really want to know,
Dorothy? Because I absolutely will tell you. Just make
sure you're gonna be OK with the answer."

I thought about that for a minute. I'd just
admitted to myself that I didn't care, but did I want to
know? "No. I mean, I'd be fine with whatever you did.
I just don't think any of them are worth another second
of my time."

Morgue rolled over to lie on top of me. He
looked down at me softly before taking my lips in a
gentle kiss. It wasn't a kiss to build sexual pleasure,
though I always found myself getting wet when he

kissed me. It was a claiming kiss. One that told me how much he treasured me. I thought he might even love me. I got the feeling he didn't love often, and I desperately wanted to be in that circle of family.

"You're a remarkable woman, Dorothy. I'm proud you're mine."

"Me too. I mean, I'm glad I'm yours." I smiled but then it faded. "What happens now? I know you got the information you wanted. What will you do with it?"

He shrugged. "That's up to Sting, but we typically hunt down these trafficking rings and kill everyone we can find."

"But you're always careful?" It wasn't a statement. I wanted that reassurance. Morgue happily gave it to me.

"Always, honey. Sting determines which missions are worth the risk and if they are, if the risk is acceptable. Then we all work to make the risk even less by preparing for every possible outcome we can imagine. There will always be danger in something like that, but we minimize it as much as we can."

"Good. Because even though I don't want to risk you getting hurt, I don't want another woman to have to go through what I did. Or worse." I frowned. "Why do you think they didn't sell me as long as I was there?"

"Wylde is looking deeper into the whole nest of vipers, but he thinks they were holding out for a better price. I know that sounds harsh, but it saved you worse trauma than what you had to endure."

"I know." I kissed him again because I had to. If I lived with this man a hundred years, I doubted I'd ever tire of his kisses. "So, it will be a while before you have to do anything else?"

"Yeah. I won't let anything slip up on you, Dorothy. I'll give you as much notice as I can if I have to leave. And I swear to you, I'll do everything in my power to always be home to you within a day. Especially until you get used to the club."

"I appreciate it. Blossom said I could borrow Sparkle any time I needed her."

Morgue grinned at me. "Speaking of Sparkle, I have something for you."

He stood and slung on some pants. I reached for my T-shirt -- which was really Morgue's shirt -- and slipped it over my head. "Wait here," he said, his face bright with excitement. I'd never seen this side of Morgue before. It was almost an oxymoron, Morgue looking happy.

He left the room and came back a few moments later with the absolutely most adorable dog I'd ever seen.

"Oh, my God! Who is this?" I reached for the dog. He happily wiggled from Morgue's arms to mine. The little hellion licked my face like he'd found a long-lost friend. The thing's little tail was wagging up a storm. It might have weighed eight or ten pounds and had long, wiry hair. His face, feet, and tail were darker than his body. And he looked familiar. "What kind of dog is he?"

"A Cairn Terrier." Morgue grinned. "Name's Toto."

I froze, then blinked at the dog. "Well. No wonder you look familiar." I giggled. Toto barked once, his tail still wagging.

That night, Morgue explained about the club tattoo and all it meant. I could never leave him or the MC. Which was fine by me. I never wanted to be away from Morgue. He said we'd get with Ace, who'd help us design the tattoo. Apparently, the women of Iron Tzars were tattooed the same as the men. Since I was an old lady now, I got a special one. The men had all agreed to get ring tattoos on their left ring finger to symbolize their wedding rings and as a show of solidarity with the women who got their property tattoos as well as their property vests. I'd like to say I was disturbed at the thought of being someone's property, but honestly, I *was* Morgue's property. Just like he was mine.

As we lay in bed after making love again, we watched the sun set through the bedroom window. It dipped behind the hills in a dazzling display of pinks, purples, and oranges. I couldn't help but wonder what my future held. One thing I knew for sure, Morgue would be at my side. Through thick and thin, in sickness and in health, to the grave do us part. And beyond. And I couldn't be happier about it.

With Morgue, I could survive *anything*.

Deacon (Iron Tzars MC 12)
A Bones MC Romance
Marteeka Karland

Apple -- I gave Deacon my heart, but he said I was too young. So he left. For over a year. Didn't want me around. Hurt and humiliated, I left for Grim Road MC. If anyone will understand my need to hide and lick my wounds for a while, it'll be my sister Lemon. Of course, Lemon's also a royal bitch. When I get shot, first thing she does is call Deacon -- the last person I ever want to see again. Then she sics him on the man who ordered the hit. Not sure who I'm gonna kill first -- Deacon, or Lemon.

Deacon -- All I ever wanted was to keep Apple safe. To protect her. Mostly from me. When my president sent me to infiltrate a trafficking ring, I gladly accepted the assignment. I thought once I was gone, Apple'd have time to grow up. Fall in love with someone her own age. Someone better. Then my enemies went after Apple. When Lemon tells me she's been shot, her call pushes me over the edge. Now, I'm going to unleash hell. Maybe then, Apple will forgive me for pushing her away.

Prologue

Apple
One Year Ago

I was so nervous I thought I might throw up. Deacon had promised to make me his old lady when I turned eighteen. That birthday had been exactly a year ago, and still he kept putting me off. Tonight, I planned on making him follow through. I knew he thought I needed time to grow up, get some life experience under my belt but I knew I wanted to be with Deacon.

I raised my hand and knocked on Deacon's door before I could change my mind again. He still lived in the clubhouse, though Sting had given him his own house in anticipation of him claiming me. We'd decorated it together, but he hadn't moved in and I hadn't either. I wasn't sure what he was waiting on, but it seemed like he was reluctant to take that last step. It wasn't that I thought he didn't want me so much as it felt like he was pulling back, yet holding me tight all at the same time.

Seconds later, Deacon opened the door.

"Hi, baby." He grinned at me, stepping back so I could enter. He shut and locked the door, then turned around and opened his arms to me. "Come here."

I grinned, leaping into his arms and wrapping my legs around his waist. Deacon found my lips with his and kissed me like he meant it. It was all I could do to contain my excited squeal. This was it. Tonight. I wanted this with everything in me!

Deacon thrust his tongue between my lips expertly, making my belly quiver and my pussy ache. I think I'd loved Deacon from the first moment I met him. I'd let him think me and Lemon were eighteen and he'd gotten just past first base. Or, rather, I guess I should say *I'd* gotten just past first base with him. Because Deacon had known something was up and kept things pretty simple. Yeah. That had gotten me a good lecture.

Being in his arms was like the beginning of a beautiful adventure. I was so excited to finally be able to follow him where I thought we both wanted to go. I wasn't naive enough to think he'd been a saint. The man was in his late twenties, and I'd just turned nineteen. I wanted him to show me everything. Where he led, I followed.

"You always taste so sweet, Applejack." I had to smile at his nickname for me. Only he called me that, and only in private. It was ours.

"Mmm..." I lost any doubt Deacon loved me with one sweep of his tongue. His arms were so strong around me, like armor keeping the whole world out if I didn't want it inside.

I could feel his cock pressed against his jeans, rubbing against my clit with every move we made. For the first time, I embraced all the sensations of pleasure and need and hunger roiling inside me. Always before, I knew we had to stop. I wasn't old enough and Deacon was too good a man to have claimed me before I was. But today...

"I don't want to wait, Deacon," I whispered. "Not anymore."

"Me neither, baby. But I've gotta give you your property patch in front of the club. You also gotta get inked."

"But --" He silenced me with a kiss before laying me down on the bed and covering me with his heavy body. His actions belied his words. I found the ridge of his cock and rubbed myself against him.

"No, Apple." His tone was stern, but he

continued to kiss me, nipping at my jaw and neck before placing a lingering kiss to the swell of my breast. He stood, reaching for me and pulling me to my feet. "Not until I give you the vest." He grinned. "And not in the clubhouse. We're goin' home." He cupped my face and kissed me once more before unlocking the door and pulling me after him back to the common room.

Deacon grinned, draping an arm over my shoulders possessively. He looked proud to have me with him. Several of the guys clapped him on the shoulder good-naturedly and gave me a nod of acknowledgement. The Iron Tzars might be as wild as any other MC, but they were respectful of their women. Besides, everyone knew Lemon would have their balls if they weren't. Also, Wylde would likely have done his worst. He might be the tech guy, but Wylde was more than what he showed on the surface.

"Deacon!" Roman called to him from across the room. The party had started, though the place was more sedate than I'd seen in the past. Especially since me and Lemon were the guests of honor, so to speak. I was sure that was why there were only a couple of club girls in the area, and they were there strictly to keep the food coming when Iris told them.

Deacon raised his hand to the enforcer. Instead of a welcoming smile, however, Roman looked serious. Like he was displeased in the extreme.

"Deacon? What's wrong?" I gripped Deacon's hand in both of mine, looking up at him. There was a look of dread briefly before his expression closed off. I glanced back at Roman who was giving Deacon a hard look in return.

"Nothin', Applejack," he murmured, leaning close to my ear. "I'll be right back." Deacon kissed my temple as he wrapped his arms around me in a fierce hug. He strode to Roman, who took him into Sting's office and shut the door. It was over an hour before the three of them exited the room. Roman said something to Deacon, who nodded. Sting gripped Deacon's shoulder, before slapping it in a show of solidarity and encouragement. Whatever had happened couldn't be too bad. Right?

Deacon scanned the room until he found me. He flashed a tight smile before heading in my direction. Once he reached me, he pulled me back into his arms and hugged me tightly for several long seconds.

"What's going on?"

"I'll explain in a minute. Let's go home first."

"Right now? The party's just started." I grinned up at him. Unease had settled in my belly. I knew something was wrong and wasn't sure I wanted to go with him right now. The longer I put off leaving, the longer I had this one night with him. Because I knew something was about to happen I wouldn't like.

"I'm sorry, honey. This can't wait." He gave me a sad, gentle look, but I could see the truth in his eyes.

I shook my head. "I don't want to, Deacon."

He closed his eyes and let out a slow breath. Gripping my hand firmly, he tugged me after him. When we got to the parking lot, he led me to his bike and climbed on. "Ride with me, Applejack." He held out his hand for me to grip for balance if I wanted to climb on. He almost willed me to take his hand.

As if I could deny him anything. I loved Deacon.

He rode me around the property for a while. I always loved the feeling of the wind in my hair as he sped over the hard paths. It felt like I was flying. The one time I'd been on the open road with Deacon especially. Even with a helmet, I'd never felt more free in my life.

All too soon the ride ended and Deacon pulled up outside the little house we'd been given. I should have been excited. This was the moment I'd been waiting for. To be at the house with the intention of having sex with Deacon. Only, I knew that wasn't going to happen. He hadn't given me his property cut. So, whatever came next wasn't going to be welcomed.

He helped me remove my helmet and lashed it to the back of his bike. Then he took my hand and we went inside. Deacon locked the door but stood with his hands on the door, his forehead against the wood.

Carefully, I placed a hand on his back. "What's going on, Deacon?" My voice was so soft I wasn't sure if he'd heard me, but after letting out a deep breath, Deacon turned to face me.

"You know I love you, right, Apple?"

I nodded. "Yes. I know."

"Then I need you to trust me. I'm going to have to wait to give you your property cut."

"Why?" I tried to keep my voice steady, but I was very near tears. "This was the plan. We were going to be together."

"We will be, Apple. I just need a year. One year. Use it to spend time with your sister doing stuff young women your age normally do."

"What is this, Deacon? I don't want to go on trips or to parties unless it's with you."

"Honey, there is something I have to take care of. It's going to require I be gone a lot over the next several months. I don't think it's fair to ask you to wait for me."

"Wait…" Dread washed through me and I shook my head. "Are you… are you breaking up with me?"

"One year, Apple. Give me a year. If you haven't

found someone you want more than me, I'll be home and I'll beg you to take me back."

"Are you going to be with other women?"

"Honey, I swear to you, I've not been with another woman since I made a commitment to you. Not in the whole three years since I've known you. That's not going to change. Not as long as you're not in a relationship."

I watched him for a long time, studying his expression. His eyes. Looking for anything that might give me some hint as to what was going on. I found nothing.

With a sigh, I nodded. "I'll be waiting on you when you come home. I don't want this to be the end."

He gave me a gentle smile. "It won't. I promise."

"Why did you want us to come here? If you're not giving me your cut yet, are we still, uh, are we going to sleep together?"

"We're not going to have sex tonight, honey. But I want to spend the night with you. I want to hold you all night while you sleep."

"We can still make love, Deacon. I want you."

"I want you too, honey. But I have to leave in the morning. I'm not sure when I'll be back, and even when I am, I might not be able to stay long. I'm not using this as an excuse to take what I want without committing to you." He cupped my face in both his hands, leaning over to brush a tender kiss over my lips. "I'm going to hold you while you sleep. You're going to give me this one night. After I leave, we'll revisit us in a year."

"I'll wait, Deacon. Just… try to talk to me as much as you can? Make sure to see me whenever possible?"

He smiled reassuringly at me. "I promise to do

everything possible to stay in contact with you, Applejack."

I took him at his word. He held me all night long. With Deacon wrapped around me, I'd never slept so well as I did that night. Sure, I woke occasionally, but only to shift my position. Always, Deacon whispered softly to me until I dozed back off. It was paradise.

* * *

The next few months, Deacon called me at least once a week. Then it backed off to once every other week. By the time our year was up, I hadn't talked to him the entire last two months before he'd promised he'd be home.

It was another two months before he finally came back to Iron Tzars MC. When he did, Deacon wasn't the same person he'd been when he'd left.

Chapter One

Deacon

I was about to do the most horrible thing I'd ever done in my life. I'd hoped Apple had found someone her own age who would adore her and treat her like the princess she was. She hadn't. And I hadn't been able to keep my promises to her. Any of them.

I couldn't be with her. I couldn't make her my old lady. Not because I didn't want to, but because I'd made some enemies. Bad ones. Granted, I'd done exactly what I'd had to, exactly what Sting had asked of me. Now I was out of that hellhole. But some of the primary players were still alive. If I was found, it wouldn't be just me who'd suffer. Apple would too. Probably more than me, because they'd use her to torture me.

Sting and I had spoken at length about this. Apple absolutely could not be around me. The enemies I'd made might hesitate to attack the compound itself, but if they knew I had a woman here, they'd throw everything they could at us and more than just the men would be in danger. Every single woman and child would be at risk. If Apple were here, they'd be in even more danger because everyone in the club would give their lives to protect one of their own.

No. The only choice was to send Apple to Riviera Beach to stay with her sister at Grim Road MC. The only way to get Apple to go willingly, was to make it so uncomfortable for her to be in the compound with me that she left on her own. If she knew I was trying to protect her, she'd not only get her sister to kick my ass, but she'd refuse to leave my side. I couldn't leave her that option.

Yeah. I was going to hell because the second I

pulled through the gates and into the parking lot in front of the clubhouse and saw Apple, I knew from the look on her face what I was about to do to her would devastate her beyond any repairing our relationship later. Apple loved me as much as I loved her. But it wasn't safe for me to be with her. Might never be. No matter the pain to her heart now, at least she'd be safe.

"Deacon!" She waved at me, jumping up and down excitedly. I couldn't help but grin. God, I'd missed her! I'd been in hell the last three months and thoughts of her had been the only thing that kept me going.

"Apple." I gave her a wide grin, resisting the urge to open my arms so she could fling herself at me like I knew she wanted to. "It's good to see you."

She gave me a hesitant smile, obviously trying to decide what to do next. I could see she was unsure of herself. It gutted me to know this was my fault. And it was going to get worse. "I've been waiting for you. I-I was afraid something had happened when you didn't show up a couple months ago."

I shrugged, giving her a fond look. I tried to make it like an uncle might look at a favorite niece, hoping she'd sense the difference in me and at least have an idea things were going to change before I laid it all out for her. "I had things to take care of… some things for the club. Sometimes it can't be helped."

"I know," she said softly, still looking up at me shyly. "When Wylde told me you were coming home today, I'd hoped we could spend the evening together."

I winced. "Sorry, honey. I'll give a report to Sting, then I really need some time to decompress." I laid a gentle hand on her shoulder and hoped like piss I wasn't shaking. The shock of touching her was bad enough. My gut was gnawing at me and my heart was truly breaking. I knew it was the right thing to do, but I wasn't sure I could go through with this. "We'll talk in a couple of days."

She jerked back like I'd struck her. This was it. I had to do it here in the common room. Not because I wanted one of my brothers to end up with her, but because I knew doing this in public would be the one thing that would cause her to run from me and not insist on staying. She could move on with her life easier if she were with her sister where her home would be hidden. Secret. She'd be with Lemon and the rest of Grim Road, and I could concentrate all my time on eliminating this bastard, Borris Illivitch.

"What do you mean?" She shook her head slightly. "Decompress? Don't you want to spend some time with me? I can maybe give you a massage."

I laughed, reaching out to ruffle her hair like I might a child's. "Sorry, squirt. We can hang out in a few days."

"Hang out." She gave me a dazed, blank look and I inwardly winced. Confusion warred with disbelief as she took a step away from me, shaking her head.

"Look." I took a step toward her. Everything inside me was rebelling, but I had to do this. I'd discussed it with Sting and he hadn't exactly agreed, but knew it was better for Apple if she were away from here for a while. Until this whole fucking mess was cleaned up for good. I had to send Apple to Grim Road where she'd be hidden. And safe. I was going to catch hell for this later, but I knew there would be no reasoning with Apple.

When it came to people she loved, Apple was just as protective as her sister, and she loved with her whole heart. Unless I gave her a good hard shove, she would never leave. Not as long as she thought we'd eventually be together. I'd wanted it to be true, but I think, deep down, I'd known even a year ago it would come to this. "I know what I said, Apple. I'm sorry. I should never have led you on."

Apple sucked in a breath, her hand fluttering over her throat defensively. "What?" Her voice was a mere thread of sound. Also, the whole of the clubhouse in the immediate vicinity was witness to everything I was saying. "What do you mean, led me on?"

I sighed. "We can't be together, Apple. We're just too different. I'm too old, and you're way the fuck too young." I patted her shoulder awkwardly. Time to deliver the killing blow. Then I really would be condemned to the seventh pit of hell. "You're a beautiful woman, Apple. But you're just not ready to take on a man like me."

I braced myself for her tears, for the accusing looks from her and every single one of my brothers in the room. It seemed like the air was all sucked out of the clubhouse and every eye was on us. Out of the corner of my eye, I saw even Sting had emerged from his office, a shocked look on his face. Yeah, everyone had picked the exact wrong moment to go silent. Well. I'd wanted everyone to witness this, to force Apple to leave. Looks like I was getting my wish.

Instead of crying, of railing at me, Apple's face went abruptly blank. The light in her eyes that I loved so much, that sparkle that told me she was happy, went out. It took every ounce of control I had not to lunge for her, to pull her into my arms and tell her I didn't mean it. That I only wanted her safe, but I'd gone too far to back out now.

"I see." She put her chin up and gave me a small

smile. "Well. I'm glad you're back safe, Deacon." She cleared her throat. "I'm sorry I misunderstood what was going on. I thought I was supposed to stay in your house, but I can see I was mistaken."

"You weren't, Apple. You're welcome to stay there as long as you like."

She shook her head. "That won't be necessary. I'll have my stuff out by the end of the day."

"I appreciate it," I said, trying to look relieved when I was dying inside. "All I want is two days' worth of sleep and to be by myself. To get my wits back." I gave her what I hoped was a tired, embarrassed smile. "Been a long year, honey."

"Yeah. I guess it has." She smiled again. "Well. Give me a few hours. I'll have Wylde let you know when the place is ready." A subtle jab? Yeah. Wylde would make my life miserable for sure. I wouldn't blame him.

Sting had agreed to keep my situation to himself unless he had to get the Tzars involved. He'd given me the original mission, but I'd cut myself off from him when he'd tried to pull me out. Everything that happened later had been my own fault.

But it had been worth it. I had a lead on two cells in a sophisticated human trafficking highway. The end of that road was about three and a half hours or so south of Corpus Christi, Texas, in Mexico. Sting said we'd start there. After that, we'd backtrack the fuckers to the start. Then we'd shut them down for good.

Now, I had to live with the consequences of my actions. That meant giving up Apple. I'd sacrificed for my country before. For my club. But this was harder than anything I'd ever imagined.

As I watched Apple saunter out of the clubhouse, I stumbled backward, leaning against a pool table for several seconds before stomping out of the common room and up to my room in the clubhouse. Once in my room, I went to the window to look outside. I knew exactly which way Apple would go and my gaze found her unerringly.

She walked in the direction of the little house Sting had given to us, not hurrying, head held high. A queen surveying her kingdom. There was no outward sign she was hurting, but I could see it in every single step she took. I knew this woman better than I knew myself. I'd cut her to the bone. The wound would eventually heal, but the scar it left behind would never go away.

And I knew any chance I had at a happy ever after just walked out of my life. For good.

Chapter Two

Apple
Four Months Later

My ears rang and my chest and shoulder hurt like a motherfucker. Everything seemed like it was coming at me from inside a well. I groaned but it sounded like my ears were plugged full of cotton and all I could hear was myself. Being shot was a motherfucking bitch. Pain meds after being shot? Also a motherfucking bitch, but better than the pain. Except for not having my wits about me.

"Oh, God…"

"Easy, honey." That voice was familiar. God, I needed out of this fog! Under other circumstances, I could see myself enjoying the feeling of floating, but I was hurting and I needed my whole brain engaged if I was going to go toe to toe with the one person I'd hoped never to see again as long as I lived.

"Go away." It was all I could manage.

"Not until I'm sure you're OK."

"I'm fine. Go away."

I didn't hear anything for a long time. I thought maybe he'd done as I told him and I wasn't sure how I felt about that. Instead, I felt a big, warm hand on my uninjured shoulder.

"Bullet's on his way with some pain meds. Just hang in there for me."

"No more meds." I shook my head, but it just made everything worse. "No more fruit punch either."

"Let Bullet decide what you need, honey. OK?" He didn't acknowledge the fruit punch and I didn't expound, but I'd found the combination of the pot-laced drink and opioids should never be a thing. It was fine as long as I was content to lie still and just enjoy the buzz, but there was no way I could function. And yeah. I might not have told Bullet I'd had the fruit punch in addition to the codeine he'd given me. My bad.

"As long as you go away."

"Apple..."

"No, Deacon. I said go away. Leave. Now." Even as I said it, my heart felt like it was being ripped from my chest. I couldn't even see him properly. My vision seemed tunneled and more than a little blurry. I tried to tell myself that was great. The last thing I needed was to see him clearly. The man I was so in love with it hurt.

It was like an affliction. I didn't want to love him. I wanted to hate him. Even knowing I'd never be what he wanted, I still loved him. I was afraid he'd be the only man I'd ever love and that, more than anything, terrified me.

"Pain gettin' bad, Apple?" That was Bullet. I turned my head -- slower this time -- to where I thought he should be. I got a blurry blob that was roughly Bullet's size. I guess.

"Yeah. But don't give me anything else."

Bullet chuckled. "I take it the fruit punch in combination with the strong pills was a little much."

I grimaced. "You'd guess right."

"If you hadn't done both of them, you'd have been better off."

"You knew about that, huh." It wasn't a question. Which, yeah. Bullet knew everything about his patients.

"Yep. Not recommended and I'd never give you the combination on purpose, but considering what you'd been through, I thought it would knock your ass out and you'd sleep." He grinned. "I never mix the fruit punch so strong it would hurt you if you took something else with it."

"If I wasn't in pain it might be kinda fun. Right now, with the fuzzy head, the pain is kind of making me sick. I don't think I could even pick up a glass of water to take a pill right now." My words were slightly slurred and I was sure a little stilted. "Christ," I muttered. "It's like there's a disconnect between my brain and my mouth. I know what I want to say but can't get it out."

"I understand." He put a bottle of water in my hand, his hand around both mine and the bottle. "I'll help you with the water if you can swallow these. Straight Tylenol. Nothing to make you even higher. Promise."

I grunted and opened my mouth. Bullet dropped in two tablets and helped me get the water to my lips. I took over from there until I'd swallowed the pills. When I trembled slightly, Bullet removed the water from my hand and set it on the table beside my bed.

"Thanks." I laid back with a groan. "If this is what it feels like to be shot, I'm not recommending it."

"I'll make sure to pass that on to everyone in the club."

"Good. Where's Lemon?"

"She and Rocket are in the middle of planning someone's death, I think." I could hear the amusement in Bullet's voice. I also knew he was completely serious.

"I hope it's some asshole named Deacon," I snarked. At least, I hope that's the way it came out. My eyes were watering and my nose running so it was possible it looked like I was crying. Na. No way.

"Heard that one was touch and go, but no. Not Deacon."

"Pity. Can you please tell the asshole in question to leave? I'm tired. I want to rest."

Bullet shrugged as he turned to Deacon. "Sorry, man. You heard the lady. And she does need rest, especially since the pot's not agreeing with her."

Deacon looked frustrated but resigned. Yeah, I could see him more clearly than I wanted to because he was just as gorgeous as I remembered. Looked a little more battle-hardened and scary, but it was still my Deacon.

"I'll be back, Apple. When I am, we need to talk."

"I think all that needed to be said was said. If it wasn't, I don't want to hear any more. You hurt me once, Deacon. I'm not game for a second round. You win."

He stared at me hard. I could tell he wanted to say something but wasn't going to. Instead, he shook his head slightly. "I'm glad you're safe, Apple. I'm sorry. For everything." He winced and shook his head again, then left the room.

I was pretty sure a piece of my soul went with him.

Bullet crouched beside the bed, patting my hand awkwardly. "Lemon thought you might want to talk to him."

My gaze snapped to Bullet's. "She thought wrong. I don't want to see him again." I made my voice as hard as I could. I wanted this point absolutely clear. Because if Deacon got to me, asked me for forgiveness, I knew I'd be helpless against him. I'd cave like a little bitch and give him whatever the fuck he wanted.

"Not a problem, honey. Cecilia is on her way. She's gonna stay with you while I finish up some clinic stuff. After that, we're both gonna stay with you."

"You don't have to do that. I'll be fine on my own."

"Not tonight, Apple. We'll talk about it tomorrow, but not while you're feeling the THC so strongly."

Yeah. I knew this wasn't a battle I was going to win. Bullet was a doctor. If he said I needed babysitting, someone was calling a fucking sitter. "Fine. But if your back aches tomorrow from sleeping on the couch, find someone who gives a fuck."

"Noted." His tone was even, but I could see his superior smirk. "I'm right in the next room if you need me. Try to get some sleep. Quickest way to get your wits back about you."

If only.

I lay back and stared up at the ceiling. Why the fuck had Lemon sent Deacon to me? Why would she think I'd even want to see the man again? Sure, she didn't know what had happened, but I knew my sister well enough to know she'd been given a version of events that had led me to Grim Road. Not from me, but from someone. My money was on Wylde. Hopefully, Deacon would respect my wishes and leave me the fuck alone. And maybe, I could finally move on.

Maybe.

I waited until I was certain Bullet was out of the room before I carefully turned over on my side so my back was facing the door. I curled up in a ball, mashed my fist against my mouth, and fucking *sobbed*.

Somehow, I'd managed to doze off. When I woke, it was with the raging need to pee and the worst case of dry mouth known to man. I sat up on the edge of the bed with a groan as my shoulder protested the movement. I attempted to stand, but my knees just weren't getting the message.

"Fuck," I muttered as I moved gingerly. I had to stand there for several seconds to see if my knees were going to hold me. Thank God they did because I was not calling out for help. I was still woozy and the whole right side of my upper body hurt like a motherfucker, but I'd handle it on my own.

Pain made taking care of business difficult, but I managed. I brushed my teeth with the toothbrush Cecilia had left for me still in the pack. I washed my face and put my hair up in a ponytail. My shoulder screamed at me, but I bit back a whimper as I dressed. The pain helped clear the last lingering effects of the THC in my system. I knew I was going to need my wits about me if I was going home before Bullet told me I could go. And that's exactly what I was going to do. I wasn't staying here where I'd last seen Deacon. Christ! It was like I could still smell Deacon in the fucking room!

I glanced out the window. It was full night outside with very little moonlight so it had to be late night or early morning. I was hoping Bullet and Cecilia would be asleep. We were still in Bullet's clinic because he had everything he needed readily available, so they were likely in one of the nearby rooms.

"He had a good reason for what he did, Apple." Lemon sat in the corner of my room, hidden in the shadows since I hadn't turned on anything other than the bathroom light.

"I'm sure he did." I shoved my feet into my shoes which, thank goodness, were slip-ons. I wasn't sure I could tie my own shoes at this point.

"You should talk to him."

"He broke my heart, Lemon." I turned away from my sister, reaching for my phone lying on the nightstand. "He left me. Not the other way around. I choose not to repeat that lesson."

"I've never asked you for anything, Apple. We always work together, each anticipating the other's needs. We always have. I'm asking you to listen to what he has to say."

"Not this time, Lemon. This isn't something you can help me with."

"I can and I am. You and Deacon belong together. Why do you think I pushed you toward him when we were sixteen? He's what you need."

"Yeah? Well, I'm not what he needs." My voice was much louder than I intended. I knew my sister, though. Unless I took a strong stand, she'd shove me in the direction she thought I needed to go whether I wanted to go or not. "I deserve better." No one but Lemon would hear the pain in my voice. My sister knew me, though. She knew how badly Deacon had hurt me even if I hadn't told her exactly what happened from my point of view.

We were both silent for a long while. When Lemon didn't say anything else, I shoved my phone in my back pocket and headed toward the door.

The clinic was dark which meant Bullet had left Lemon and Cecilia in charge of me while he got some sleep. No doubt Lemon had sent Cecilia to bed while I'd been out of it. Just meant there were fewer obstacles to me leaving.

The night air was warm and humid but not unpleasant. I took off at a brisk walk down the wide, dirt path. Rocket had given me a house near his and Lemon's so I was close to my sister, but not so close I could hear the two of them getting freaky.

Took a few minutes, but I finally made it inside my house and locked the door behind me. hurried into my bedroom and practically dove inside the closet.

When Deacon had broken things off with me, I'd used this as my safe space. A place I could decompress in private when things got too hard. There were blankets set up in the very back corner. My body screamed in protest, but I lay with my face down against the blankets and raged with all the fury, anger, and pain inside me. The blankets muffled most of the noise, but my throat was raw and aching.

For the second time tonight, I cried myself to sleep. Tomorrow. I'd deal with everything tomorrow.

Chapter Three
Deacon

It was time to go hunting. I had a fuck-ton of rage built inside me and I was going to take it out on every motherfucker who was involved with the attack on Grim Road. I didn't really care about anyone there, though I respected everyone I'd met from Grim. The only person I cared about was Apple. She was hurting both physically and emotionally and I was the cause of at least one of them. There was a good possibility me and Sting hadn't hidden my relationship with Apple as well as I'd hoped and that could have played a part, but Sting and Wylde didn't think so. And yeah, the meeting with Wylde had gone about as well as I could have expected. Which is to say I nearly got my ass beat. Again.

I had a meeting with one of the scum tonight. It was the only fucking reason I'd left Apple instead of sitting with her, no matter what her wishes had been. I needed to be near her. To know she was safe and healing. I needed to be there taking care of her. Which just pissed me the fuck off all the more.

I was done. Done. This was it. What I was about to do would get my club to cull me and rightfully so. But, by God, I was tired of this. *All* of this. Men who hurt women for the fun of it. Men who sold women and children to the highest bidder. Hell, a man like Borris Illivitch who could sell his own stepdaughter to settle his debts? None of them deserved to live. They deserved to have the same things happen to them as they sold their prey into. That was exactly what I was gonna dish out tonight.

I'd killed plenty of times since I'd joined the Marines. Even more when I'd been loaned to the CIA because I was the best hunter in service. I was young and inexperienced, but I was a go-getter. So I'd killed. So many fucking times. Never once did I leave the killing field that I didn't feel the need to puke. It's why I didn't make a career out of the military or even move on to private work with the CIA. This time, however, I was looking forward to the fucking killing.

No. That wasn't entirely true. I wasn't looking forward to the actual killing. I was looking forward to what came... before. Every single man I was getting ready to kill was going to suffer like they'd never dreamed. The fucking thing about it was, I'd never even come close to snapping like this. The mere thought that any of this had come to touch Apple -- in any way at all -- drove me to a murderous rage. Combine that with her complete and total *rightful* rejection of me and the need to go scorched earth on these men was a compulsion. It was the only thing that might come close to easing some of the anger and grief inside me.

"Easy there, brother." Falcon settled himself next to me. He kept a wary distance, eyeing me like I was a ticking time bomb. He wasn't wrong.

"Ain't your brother," I muttered as I went back to studying the yachts anchored in the marina. Big-ass boats for the ultra-rich wannabes. Borris Illivitch fell into that category. He had money, but not nearly as much as he wanted. Or needed. He was currently on that boat. And I wanted on it with him.

"Sure you are. We're Marines. That makes us brothers, right?"

I didn't even look at the guy. "Nope."

"Come on, Deacon. You don't want to go in there alone." Finally, I glanced at Falcon. The other man was quartering the area like a pro. I knew he'd be a good man to have at my back. I also knew he was only here because Rocket wanted to make sure I didn't make a mess in his territory. He didn't care if the guy died. He just didn't want anything to lead back to his club or any of his men. Which was fine. I got it. But when I hunted, I went alone. Always. Which is why Falcon would soon find out he wasn't going any-fucking-where.

"Yeah, Falcon. I'm going in by myself. Don't want or need you to have my back." I moved, sitting up and fiddling with my go bag while Falcon continued to study the boat and area around it. He really should pay attention to his immediate surroundings. After this lesson, he would from now on.

"Tough shit, bro. Got orders I'm to stay on your six." Falcon didn't take his eyes from the boat. He had field glasses up now.

I glanced at my watch. It was synced with Wylde's and he was switching off all security cameras in exactly fifteen seconds. "Then stay on my six. Way the fuck back on my six." I stood and moved toward the pier. Falcon... didn't.

"The fuck, Deacon," he hissed. Which was good, 'cause if he'd given me away, I'd fucking shoot him and deal with the fallout later. "Get the fuckin' cuff off my ankle."

I turned and grinned at him. "Stay put, sunshine."

Falcon continued to sputter but he did it quietly so he got to live. Not that I cared much. I just didn't want that bastard, Borris, having a fucking heads-up he was being hunted.

Getting on the yacht was surprisingly easy. I'd expected guards and was ready, but the kids had no idea what they were doing. Not only that, but they were light with only two men on the gangway, one inside, and the captain. Taking them out was easy.

Once the captain was knocked out, I dragged all the men off the boat and secured them on the pier. Falcon would get loose eventually and take care of them because he didn't have much of a fucking choice. Then I made a round on the boat. Borris, the fucker, was passed out in his cabin. What I assumed was cocaine lay in messy lines on a mirror beside the bed. Bastard must have been completely wasted.

I tied him down quickly enough. Fucker just kept snoring. Once I was sure the place was secure, no one else on board, I took the boat out to sea. What I was getting ready to do was going to take some time. And be very noisy. And messy.

The boat had a personal water craft docked, full of gas, and ready to run. Once I was done, I'd anchor the yacht in Davy Jones's Locker. I just had to make sure I didn't go so far I didn't have enough gas to get back to shore. Which was something I'd trained for and knew very well how to do.

I gave it a few hours. Not only did I want Illivitch good and sober when we started, I needed to rest. Though it had taken little effort to dispatch the guards and the one crew member, I'd been awake for close to forty-eight hours and needed my wits about me. Borris wasn't going anywhere.

I lay down on a bench in the wheelhouse. It was actually quite comfortable. With the ocean gently rocking the boat and the sound of waves hitting the sides, it was easy to drift off.

I woke to the sounds of Borris Illivitch yelling at the top of his lungs, angry as shit. Yeah. He was good and pissed. He had no idea exactly what kind of trouble he was in or he'd be sobbing in fear. Oh well. There was time enough for that later.

I got to my feet and headed below deck where I'd left Illivitch. Sitting on the top step, was Falcon.

"Christ," I swore, kicking the other man half-heartedly so he had to catch himself before he tumbled below deck. "What the fuck are you doin' here, man?"

"Rocket's orders. Do what you want to the bastard, but I'm here on behalf of Grim Road. You do this in our territory, it becomes our business."

"You're here to babysit me, motherfucker. I don't need it."

"No?" He raised an eyebrow. "Seems to me you do. Besides, I got a better boat than that pissy little water scooter." He stood, leaning against the railing. "You *do* plan on sinkin' the fuckin' boat. Right?"

"I don't fuckin' need this," I muttered, scrubbing a hand over my face. "Stay or go. Don't give a fuck. But stay out of my fuckin' way."

Without waiting for an acknowledgment, I descended the ladder. Illivitch's quarters were in the aft of the ship at the end of the passageway. Illivitch's angry shouts bellowed from behind the door.

I shoved the door open and sneered at the man tied to the bed. "Well, well, well. What do we have here?" Cliché, but I didn't give a fuck. The more painful I could make it for this man the better satisfied I'd be. Which included cheesy villain lines.

"I'll fuckin' kill --" He stopped mid-sentence as he got a good look at me. "D-Deacon? What the fuck?" Yeah. Motherfucker had a right to be nervous. He knew what I was capable of.

"I warned you. I let you go before because you were of more use to me alive than dead, but I found out that was a mistake on my part. One I won't repeat."

"I haven't done anything, Deacon." He lifted his chin and tried for an air of authority, like he fully expected me to not only believe him but release him immediately.

"Oh? What about your stepdaughter?"

He gave me a lascivious grin. "She's a hot little bitch, isn't she? Perfectly legal. She's not my daughter, and she's over eighteen. You can have her if you want. She was a virgin when she ran off so, even if one of those bikers did fuck her, she's not been used too much. Just let me go and I'll let you do whatever you want to her. Only thing I ask is that you bring her back in one piece and unscarred." This guy!

"You really are a dumbass," I chuckled, crossing my arms over my chest. "You don't have Calista, Borris. Even if you did, it's this very thing right here that's gettin' you killed." I yanked the bedding off him and took out my knife. He flinched back, but I just started cutting off his clothes. "You're telling me --" I kept my tone as conversational as I could, "-- you're willing to give me your stepdaughter, the young woman your beloved wife left in your care after she passed away, to use how I please. To fuck the shit outta her whether she wants it or not."

He scoffed. "You know as well as I do bitches like her always want it. They tease us, then get all pissy when we take what they're offering. Calista is just like all the rest of 'em. She won't care. She'll pretend she doesn't want it, but she'll secretly get off on it." He gave me a cajoling smile. "I'll have her back with me any day now. She's fuckin' some guy in a biker gang around here. Girl loves slummin'. Give her a few days to rest up and I'm sure her pussy will be just as tight and hot as it ever was."

Without a word, I continued to cut off his clothes until he was completely nude. As I thought, he was aroused. Likely from fantasizing about all the things that would happen to Calista. Sick fuck.

"So, a couple things." I sheathed my knife and shrugged out of the small backpack I had over my shoulders and set it at the foot of the bed. "First off, Calista is perfectly fine and well. She's with her daddy's enforcer. And Ringo isn't the kind of man to let an attack on his woman go without consequences." I grinned as I watched Borris's expressions go from surprise to fury in the space of only a few seconds.

"Motherfuckers!" His explosion wasn't unexpected. Fucker was crazy and had fixated on Calista. Knowing he was beaten was bound to push him over the edge. "She's mine!"

"No. She's Ringo's. Which brings us to the second thing. When you sicced Redwood on Calista, you forgot to tell him not to shoot anyone."

"What the fuck do I care who he shoots?"

"Because he missed Calista and hit another woman."

"Bitch shoulda been out of the way." Borris stuck his chin up, like he was daring me to contradict him.

"Right," I drawled, digging into my bag and pulling out several large dildos and a jar of ghost pepper sauce I'd use for lube. "See, here's the problem I have, Borris. You're a predator. You prey on women. You haven't gotten to children yet, but you're flirting with it. It's why you needed to sell Calista. Right? To pay for the little boy you wanted?"

Illivitch froze, his eyes wide. Like he just realized a hellhound was staring at him from the foliage. "What do you want?" His voice was a raspy whisper. Yeah. He knew he was fucked.

"I want you to die, Borris. It's really that simple." I shrugged. "The more complicated part is how you die. And how long it takes."

"Anything, Deacon." Illivitch was sweating now, his breathing shallow and rapid. Yeah. He knew this wasn't going to go well for him. "Name your price!" God, I loved hearing him beg for mercy. It would do him no good, but I wanted to drag it out. To make him suffer like he made others suffer.

"You're going to tell me who you move skin to. I want every single name. When I'm convinced you've given me everything you know, we'll discuss how you die."

"I don't know their names," he snapped, angry once again. He probably thought I'd cave and let him go. He really should have known better. I'd told him as much when I let him go before. Guess he didn't believe me. Well. He was about to find out just how wrong he was. "None of them! Everything's done anonymously for this very reason."

I gave him a look of false sympathy. "I was afraid you'd say that." I grinned at him. "Just as well we do things the hard way. I think you should get a taste of what you dish out." I tossed a giant latex dick onto his belly. "I got all kinds of shit in my bag o' goodies. I promise. You're gonna love this every bit as much as those women you sold did." I shrugged. "Maybe even more because I'm an overachiever."

"What? What are you gonna fucking do?"

"Shit." I chuckled. I was actually amused at how he was trying to deny what he knew was about to happen. "Surely to God, even you ain't that fuckin' stupid."

I expected him to come off with something else like, "You can't do this," or "You'll never get away with this." But he just whimpered, trying to move his legs together where I had them tied, spread eagle, to the bed.

"Oh good," I said with a bright smile. "I see you get it now. Feel free to scream as much as you like."

I drew out the torture for several days. Figured it was no less than the fucker deserved. Surprisingly, Falcon didn't protest. He didn't help in the actual torture, but he got in more than a few good licks. It was his club that had been affected by this bastard as I understood. I could tell some of the things I'd done to Illivitch had gone way past his comfort zone. He hadn't protested once, though.

I used a secure satellite link to get the information I'd gotten out of Illivitch to Wylde, who promised to have me a hunting destination in twenty-four hours. That was on the sixth day. Falcon objected to more but only because he said the food stores on the boat were out and he wanted a fucking pizza. I didn't have much of an appetite but I could sympathize. And not because of the mess I'd made of Illivitch. Apple was at the Grim Road compound and she didn't want me with her. I wasn't going to listen to her, but it still made me feel a little dead inside knowing how much I'd hurt her. And that she could have died because I wasn't there to protect her.

"Time to go," I said. Borris was conscious but barely coherent, and only because I'd taken great pains to not let him pass out. Was hard though. His genitals and anus were in very sorry shape. Only thing I regretted was having to touch the fucker. Thank Christ for surgical grade personal protective equipment because not only was there blood everywhere, the last thing I'd wanted to actually touch was this guy's junk. "I'd just let you drown or be shark bait, but I don't like loose ends. Rot in hell, you bastard." I cut his throat and watched as he finished bleeding out. Too easy as far as I was concerned, but he'd still suffered. It would have to be enough for me. For now anyway. Once I found these other bastards, however, I'd see if I could refine my technique and keep them alive for weeks.

"Boat's ready whenever you are, Deacon," Falcon said casually before adding, "Remind me never to piss you off. I think I'd rather deal with Lemon."

"Some things need to be done. If you think Lemon wouldn't do the same thing I just did in the same situation, you don't know your vice president very well."

"Point taken."

"Let me set the charges on the hull and we can blow this joint."

Falcon snorted out a laugh. "You're gonna fit right in with that family."

I stilled. "What family?"

"Lemon and Apple. You're exactly like them. Inappropriate humor and mean as fuck."

"I'm not their family, Falcon. They ain't mine."

"No? That ain't what Lemon said."

"Lemon was wrong."

"Uh-huh." Falcon clapped me on the shoulder. "Let me know how that works out for you."

Chapter Four

Apple

I watched from the clubhouse common room as Falcon and Deacon pulled into the compound. Deacon climbed off his bike and stalked inside. There was an intense anger about him. Something I'd never seen from him before. It was like he was a whole different person. He barely even looked like the man I knew. This man was dangerous.

He went straight to Rocket's office with Falcon following at a slower pace. Falcon glanced in my direction and held my gaze. I tilted my head, narrowing my eyes as I studied him. Falcon just shook his head slightly but continued to Rocket's office. Whatever had happened wasn't good.

I shifted where I'd been reclining on one of the sofas. As a rule, I didn't spend a lot of time on the furniture inside the clubhouse unless it was wooden. Lord only knew whose snatch or spunk would be on anything cloth. But Lemon had had some new furniture set up in one corner of the common room for the old ladies and anyone female who was not a club whore. Double standard maybe, but a line was a line and this was mine.

I sat up and winced as the right side of my torso protested the movement. It had been a week since I'd been shot and I was healing nicely, but I was still in pain and refused anything other than over-the-counter painkillers. I worked through it, breathing away the discomfort as I stood and followed the men to Rocket's office.

Lemon was leaning with her hip against the open door, her arms crossed over her chest as she listened to Deacon and Falcon report on what had happened.

"Illivitch is dead. Boat's scuttled about twenty miles offshore," Deacon said. "Wylde and your boys Crush and Byte did some diggin' and found the guards and the captain of the boat were willing accomplices, so they died too."

Rocket glanced sharply at Falcon who just shrugged. "All taken care of, Prez. No bodies to find."

"Crush said you gave them a list of names to track down." Rocket sat back, tapping a pen against a pad of paper on his desk absently. "They all connected?"

Deacon nodded. "A few months ago, Iron Tzars rescued some women from a shithole in Mexico. It was the result of over a year of hunting those fuckers. Most of the women didn't make it. With the information we got that led us to that place and the stuff I'd learned over the last year, we knew there were a few stops along the way for most of the girls. A highway that leads from Appalachia to Mexico." Deacon shrugged. "Little out of our territory, but with skin trafficking, borders get blurry."

"We do the same. It's why we're all here now." Rocket nodded for Deacon to continue.

"When I questioned Illivitch, I got two other names. The list I made for the tech guys is made up of those two guys and their associates. Men and women who work for them regularly in any capacity from the trafficking to the lawn service. We're gonna look into every one of them and find the next rung in this never-ending ladder. We'll likely never get them all, but we can chip away at it."

Rocket was silent for a long time. I came up beside Lemon who looped her arm through mine. She didn't hesitate to show affection in front of the guys, but not usually when they were discussing club business. Normally, this would be something they'd take behind closed doors, but since Grim Road wasn't officially involved, I guess they didn't consider it club business. Or they just didn't care who knew.

"Did you infiltrate any major drop-off points?" Rocket steepled his fingers.

"I did," Deacon answered. "More than one. I'd just come back from that leg of the operation when…" He cleared his throat, shaking his head slightly, clearly uncomfortable with whatever he'd been about to say and changed his mind. "A few months ago." He kept his gaze straight ahead as he spoke. "But I didn't get out clean. Sting told me to abort, but I was so close to finishing what I'd started I disregarded and cut myself off from the club. It was then I confirmed Borris Illivitch had an in with these guys going straight to the top."

"What kind of setup is this, Deacon?" Brick's deep, rumbling voice was surprisingly soft. Like the subject demanded reverence and respect and he was doing his best to be gentle in his questioning.

"I can't find the head of it. But it starts with ultrarich… clients who pay top dollar for young women and/or men -- children even -- to be their personal whores, for lack of a better word. They are basically kept as sexual slaves until the master gets tired of them. Then he trades them off or sells them to someone who peddles them off to less wealthy clients. After that, they're sold to what amounts to human farms. I don't think any one place has more than fifteen or twenty men and women at a time, but they're whorehouses or have pimps who send them from client to client. Like a Fuck Me delivery service." I shivered as he continued. "This is usually as far as males get. They either get too old to be able to sell, or they've gotten killed at some other point on the line. Either way, they die."

Lemon put her arm around my shoulders and pulled me close to her. I should have known my sister would know how the account upset me. I really tried to be a hard-ass like her, but I'd always been the tender-hearted one. I was a nurturer. When someone was hurting, I needed to help. In this case, it wasn't only the faceless women and boys I felt for, but Deacon too. I would bet my life, no one else in that room could hear the anguish in Deacon's voice I did. I knew Deacon, had loved him since I was sixteen. More than four years.

I hadn't gotten to know the new Deacon, but I could see how he'd changed. And that core of him, the protective, compassionate man I'd fallen in love with, was shaken to his very soul by what he'd witnessed.

"Each stop they make is worse than the last. Along the way, each handler collects more and more girls. By the time they reach Mexico, most of them are barely human. They're completely broken."

"So you took out one house in Mexico?"

"Three," Deacon said. "The first one when we rescued Morgue's old lady. Then I came back for two more." He shook his head. "But that's just the tip of the fuckin' iceberg. I'm under no illusions we're gonna shut down this highway completely. It's too widespread with too many independent buyers. I'm just trying to get the ones we know about or find as we go. Sting doesn't want this shit in his territory and I'm sure you don't either.

"Anyway, I was compromised. I contacted Sting and told him the situation. He wasn't happy but ordered me home rather than transferring me to another chapter. We had no intention of leaving any of those fuckers alive anyway, so, even though there was danger as long as they were alive, we knew they wouldn't be alive long. Unfortunately, things got hot fast. They got out of hand and..." He held out his hands to his sides. "Here we are."

"What's your next move?" Rocket's question was more of a demand.

"Just waiting for Wylde to find the two people I'm looking for. Supposed to be in this area. If I can find them, I can shake loose more of this network."

"He got Byte and Crush lookin' too?"

"Yeah. I think so. At least, they knew what we were working on with Illivitch. Can't imagine Wylde not keeping them in the loop if that's what you and Sting agreed to."

Rocket gave Deacon a crisp nod. "Good. I suggest you get some rest. Sounds like you're gonna be busy for a while. Who're they looking for?"

"Guy named Martin Calhoun."

Lemon straightened. "Olivia's stepdad?"

Deacon's head whipped in my direction, his gaze fixing on me. "You know this guy?"

"He forced Olivia to agree to spy on us." Lemon looked bored but I knew she was anything but. "He was going to give Olivia to his wealthy clients as a sex toy. Little 'some some' for them to enjoy. You know. For a price. Guy's a billionaire. Super wealthy."

She glanced at Rocket. "Didn't I hear something about him selling and trading young women and men in a trafficking ring?" I had to suppress a shiver. The thought was repulsive, and I hoped the bastard rotted in hell whenever they found him.

"Christ." Deacon dug his thumb and finger into his eyes. "I didn't realize how hard this mess had touched you guys."

"If you're after that son of a bitch, we're goin' with you." Rocket's tone brooked no argument, but Deacon was shaking his head, a stubborn, determined look on his face.

"I work alone, Rocket. It's the way I'm built."

"You worked OK with Falcon."

"Falcon didn't work with me. He stood by, let me do my shit, then followed me out."

"This is still our territory."

"We ain't found him yet, Rocket. He might not be in your territory when we do."

"Crush and Byte have been driving them this way for the past couple of weeks."

"And your guys didn't think to say anything to Wylde?" Irritation colored Deacon's voice as he pulled out his phone, shooting off a text. Probably to Wylde.

"Can't answer to that. Obviously my tech guys didn't share it with me either until they briefed me just before this meeting." Rocket shook his head, obviously not happy to have been kept in the dark, but not complaining more.

"Probably," Lemon drawled, "because it didn't matter if you both knew until the fucker was found. Now, can we move on?"

Rocket shot her an irritated look. "You know, sometimes, I wish you were less of a smartass, Lemon."

She raised an eyebrow at her man. "Better a smartass than a dumbass."

"Christ," Brick chuckled. "Keep going, Rocket. Me and the brothers'll grab some popcorn and beer. Be one helluva time."

"You're an asshole, Brick."

Brick just grinned.

"Go get some rest, Deacon. We'll work together

on this. If you prefer to work with Falcon, since it seems you two already have an understanding, I can arrange for him to be the one with you. That way someone has your back to call in reinforcements if you run into something you can't handle.

I'll also have someone there to look after Grim Road's interests."

Deacon shook his head, but I could tell he saw merit in the idea. "I don't know. If I have a target on my back, do you really want to risk being collateral damage?"

I sucked in a breath, unable to suppress the surge of fear. For Deacon. Which pissed me all the way off, but I was too busy trying to process the first to worry about the second. "No one's gonna be collateral damage, and no one's gonna get to you, Deacon." I stomped over to him. "You will take as many people as Rocket says you need, and you won't fucking argue about it."

He tilted his head at me, narrowing his gaze. "You don't tell me how to do a job, Apple." His voice was hard and the look in his eye held a warning I knew better than to go against.

Deacon had never spoken to me in that tone of voice before. He'd also never treated me with anything but kindness and tenderness. Right up until the day he'd broken my heart. Remembering that day fueled my anger, stoking it to a fever pitch.

"You're a complete fucking asshole, Deacon. I fucking hate you!"

"Yeah, figured," he muttered, not meeting my gaze. He scrubbed a hand over his face and then the back of his neck. "Christ. I don't have fuckin' time for this shit, Apple. I need to get some rest so I'm ready to go hunting once Wylde gives me a direction."

Without thinking about it too much, I stepped close to him and slapped his handsome face. If I was hurting, he was gonna fucking hurt too.

Chapter Five
Deacon

Yeah. I deserved that slap in the face. I deserved that and way the fuck more than Apple was likely to dish out even if she did want to pretend to be a badass. I knew I'd treated her badly but leaving her alone was the best way to protect her. If it hadn't been for her being shot, I'd have stayed away completely. I wouldn't have caused her more pain, and I wouldn't have lost another piece of my heart to her.

It was easy to tell how difficult this was for her. I'd done my best to act like she didn't matter to me, like I had so many more important things to do than hang out with a girl who was several years my junior, but my entire being was focused completely on Apple.

"You're out of line, Apple."

"And you're an insufferable bastard." She bared her teeth. In that moment, she reminded me more of her sister than ever. It made me wince. Not because I didn't like Lemon or anything, but because I loved my sweet Apple. I was sorely afraid Apple would never be that same soft, caring woman again. Which was completely one hundred percent my fault. "So I guess we both have our fucking issues."

She was right up in my face, giving me a piece of her mind -- well, her face was actually level with my chest, but that was beside the point. She was fire and passion, things I'd never associated with Apple before. She was the peacekeeper, the voice of reason. Not so this version of her. This woman was a force of fucking nature. Just like her sister.

And it turned me the fuck *on*.

"I think it's time you and I came to an understanding." I grabbed her upper arm and dragged her out of Rocket's office. I wasn't sure where I was going or what I was gonna do with her when I got there, but it took me all of five seconds to realize I'd hit my limit with Apple.

"Let me go, you ape!"

"Not until we settle this between us."

"You're being an asshole!"

"And you're being a fuckin' brat!" I growled the insult at her as I dragged her down the hall. I thought I heard Lemon call out, but all I could really process was the roaring in my ears, the need to get Apple alone and in my arms paramount when I should be pushing her away. Not trying to hold her closer.

I marched down the hall to the room Rocket had given me when I'd first gotten to the compound to check on Apple. With a grunt, I shoved it open and pulled Apple in after me and slammed the door shut.

"Let go of me!" She kicked out, catching my shin. Unfortunately she was wearing flip flops so I knew it had to have hurt her more than me, but she didn't even wince. She did grimace when she tried to twist free of my grasp. It was a stark reminder that she'd recently been shot. And I'd just made her pain worse by dragging her across the clubhouse.

I let her go but stayed between her and the door. Under no circumstances was she getting out of this room before she and I came to an understanding.

"Didn't mean to hurt you, Applejack."

She let out an angry screech and launched herself at me. Her fists pummeled my shoulders and chest, but she didn't try to strike my face again. Which told me more than she likely wanted me to know. Apple didn't really want to hurt me, but she was hurting. Desperately.

"Don't call me that!" she yelled. "You don't get

to call me that ever again!"

"I know, Appleja--" I cleared my throat, stopping myself from using my nickname for her. "I know. I'm sorry."

The pain and anger on Apple's face was enough to make my heart ache and my stomach tighten. I'd done this to her. It was my fault. Didn't matter that I'd done it to keep her safe, I'd still hurt her. Diminished that light in her eyes that I'd loved since the first moment I'd seen her. For that, I might never forgive myself.

"Not sorry enough," she snapped. "You think manhandling me is going to solve anything, Deacon?"

I could see the hurt in her eyes, the way her body tensed up readying for a fight or flight response. I hated myself more in that moment than I had since the day I'd sent her fleeing from me. "I didn't think. I just..." I trailed off, unsure of how to explain the torrent of emotions driving me to drag her here like some caveman.

"You think you can force me into submission? Is that it? Any right you had to put your hands on me, for any reason, you threw away when you decided I wasn't enough for you. I left. I got out of your way like I'm sure you wanted."

"I did, Apple. I wanted you to come to Grim Road and your sister. This place is so well-hidden and protected, even the locals don't know where it is." I took a step toward her, but she mirrored my movement, dancing backward to keep distance between us now where she never had before.

Before...

Apple always ran toward me. Never away. *Before.*

Before I'd left on that mission for Sting. *Before* I'd

infiltrated this fucking trafficking ring. *Before* I'd broken her heart.

Apple's eyes flashed with a mixture of pain, anger, and something else I couldn't quite pin down. Her chest heaved in deep breaths. Her lips parted as if she was deciding on her next barrage of curses. But then, surprisingly, she went quiet. The silence stretched between us, thick and tense.

"I don't want to fight you, Deacon," she finally said, her voice low and shaking. "But I can't keep doing this... this dance where you pull me close and then push me away as if I mean nothing to you." Her gaze met and held mine. Tears glistened in her bright, blue eyes but refused to well and fall.

"I never said you didn't mean anything to me, Apple." My words came out an anguished whisper because I knew what I'd said to her and the way I'd treated her said exactly that. "You've always been the one bright spot in my life. You mean... *everything*." Telling her this was the exact wrong move, but the words were wrenched out of me. I swallowed hard, shaking my head slightly. "I pushed you away to protect you."

"Don't give me that bullshit," she snapped, a fierce scowl on her lovely face. Apple should never look like this. Displeased. Angry. Hurt. She should never have anything other than a happy, contented smile on her face because she was nothing but sweetness and light. Which was exactly why I needed to push her away. "I don't need your protection, Deacon. I never did. I've got my sister and the whole of Iron Tzars and Grim Road to protect me. Both clubs, wherever I want to make my home, will keep me safe. From anything and everything."

Apple's voice was steadier now, a hard edge

sharpening her words. "I came here on my own terms. I'm not some damsel you need to save, Deacon. I'm stronger than you think."

I ran a hand through my hair, the weight of our past and present mistakes tangling in every strand. "I know you are," I admitted, my voice hoarse with the emotion clogging my throat. "Stronger than I ever gave you credit for. But that doesn't mean I don't worry about you, that I don't want to make sure you're safe."

"No. You were looking for a way out and now you feel guilty." She gave a derisive snort. "You said for me to move on. Just because I don't want to see you dead doesn't mean I haven't done exactly what you told me to do and found someone else."

Everything inside me rebelled. I clenched my fists, growling and baring my teeth, like some kind of predator angry that another predator was in my territory. "Who?" It was a command. I wanted to know what man had touched her. So I could fucking castrate the bastard.

"None of your business. It ceased to be your business when you came back that last time." She shook her head, frowning up at me as tears now spilled from her eyes down her cheeks.

"It's every bit my fuckin' business." I was back on the edge of my control. I wasn't sure how much more I could take before I completely lost my mind. "You're mine, Apple! No one else's!"

There was silence for several beats. We stared each other down, then she scoffed at me. "Fuck you, Deacon."

The defiance in her voice pierced me with its validity. I had no counter because she was right. It wasn't my business by my own decree. Apple was strong, surrounded by people who would lay down their lives for her. Yet, the selfish part of me that hated letting her go, that despised not being the one to stand by her side and shield her from the world -- protect her, love her -- raged silently within.

Her gaze cooled to an icy calm that contrasted with the fiery defiance of moments ago. "Why did you come here, Deacon? What do you want from me?"

I couldn't answer that. Part of me wanted to believe I came back for noble reasons, to ensure her safety or maybe just to see her face. But deep down, I knew better. It was selfishness, the pure unadulterated need to have her in my sphere once more, even if it was just as a specter in her life. But I knew Apple would never settle for a ghost. She needed a flesh and blood man. Someone to protect her. Someone to cherish and spoil her. As much as I still wanted her, and thought maybe I could be what she needed once I got rid of Martin Calhoun, I knew I didn't deserve to have a second chance with her. Actually, this would probably be a third chance and that was just too much to ask of anyone.

Apple crossed her arms, her posture rigid as the wind gusted through an open window, pulling strands of her blonde hair across her face. "You always think you know what I need," she said, the resentment in her tone palpable. "But you don't, Deacon. You never did. At least not when it mattered."

"What would you have had me do, Apple? Huh?" I wanted to pull my hair out. There was a war going on inside me. One part of me knew I needed to let her go. I'd been right all those months ago. She was way too young for me. Twenty to my thirty. "I knew I was bringing danger to the Iron Tzars' gate."

"They didn't send anyone away, Deacon," she shot back. "If we'd been in that much danger, Sting would have put all the women and children on lockdown, or sent them away. Bones. Salvation's Bane. Black Reign. All of them would have offered to take everyone in. Hell, the Shadow Demons would have taken everyone in and put us in the lap of luxury, pooling all their considerable resources and manpower to get the danger away from us if Sting thought it was warranted." She thumped her chest with her fist. "You saying it was only me who was in danger? Because I won't believe it. No. You made a decision for me, without letting me be part of that decision. I'm not sure how you managed to keep it all from Lemon, but if you brought the same danger here you did to Iron Tzars, then you broke my heart for nothing!" She wailed that last part in an anguished cry.

The truth stung, more than I'd like to admit. She was right. I had made decisions for both of us without her input, thinking I knew best, thinking I was keeping her safe when in reality, I was just pushing her further away. Every choice I'd made, every action I'd taken driven by my desire to protect her had only served to harm her.

I took a slow step toward her. "You're a hundred percent right. I fucked up. I won't lie and tell you Sting was all in with what I did. The fear was that I hadn't hidden my relationship with you well enough. That someone from these cells I'd been trying to infiltrate would come after you to hurt me. I sat next to Borris Illivitch for months before I took down that first group. I looked into his eyes, listened to his depraved tales. When I was finally able to find the next link in the chain, I let him see what I was capable of. I let him live in case I needed him, but that was the biggest mistake of my life. It was what made me push you away from me."

"Still doesn't explain why you're here now. You ran me off from Iron Tzars and one sister. Do you think you can force me away from my twin too?"

"No, Apple. I've not come here for a repeat of our last meeting. Lemon called me after you were shot. I don't know how much she knows, but she told me I was an ass and that you needed me."

"Well, she was wrong. I don't need you. I'll be fine on my own."

"I'm not leavin' you again. Not now. Not ever."

"Oh, come on! You're so fucking arrogant! You think I'll... what? Take you back just like that? We were supposed to have started our life together over two years ago! I'd say you lost the right to ask to see me when you told me you needed some rest before we could hang out."

"Damnit, Apple! I'm not leaving until I know you've healed. You could have died!"

"You think I don't know that? But my actions saved Calista's life so I don't regret them. Now, while I appreciate you coming when my sister called, I don't need you here. I don't want you here."

Chapter Six

Apple

The second I uttered the words, I knew I'd made a pretty bad error. Deacon was a bastard and I hated him right now, but he also knew me better than I knew myself. As a result, he could tell when I was lying. Like I was doing right now. Because, I *didn't* not want Deacon here. Oh, no. I *desperately* wanted him here. I thought I might even *need* him here. No one had ever made me feel as safe and loved as Deacon had. *Before.* I wanted those feelings back. I needed them to feel whole again, but I wasn't sure I could ever reclaim what we'd lost.

"You're lying," he whispered. "You *do* want me here."

"You're imagining things."

"I don't think I am." He took a slow step toward me, keeping me away from the door and freedom. "You want me here."

I tried to hold his gaze, defiant, but my heart was betraying me, pounding so loudly I feared he could hear it. "You can't just walk back into my life and assume --"

"Assume what? That you still care?" His voice was low, a dangerous kind of soft that wrapped around me like a shroud. "I know you, Apple. I can see it in your eyes."

My frustration was boiling over. The nerve of the man standing before me was only matched by the undeniable pull I felt toward him. A pull just as strong today as it was the first day I met him.

"That's just it," I snapped. "You know me better than anyone ever has other than Lemon. Why does it have to be you? Why can't I love someone else? God know I'd tried, too." I'd flirted with some of the guys at Grim, just to see if there was a spark of excitement. Even if it was only about sex. But there hadn't been. No one other than Deacon would ever be what I wanted.

He advanced on me then, a mask of fury falling over his features. "There damned well better not be anyone else." He backed me up until I was against the wall. "Who is he, Apple? Who the fuck is he?"

OK. This was new. I'd never seen Deacon lose his cool like this. His eyes were wild with both anger and… pain? I decided to ignore the emotional outburst and answer the question as if he didn't look like a crazy person.

"None of your Goddamned business, Deacon. You don't even get to ask that question, let alone get an answer."

"No? Fine. Your decision. But I'm gonna make sure you know who you belong to now."

Before I could protest and tell him to go fuck himself, Deacon brought his mouth down on mine and kissed me like he was fucking *starving* for me.

The kiss was both an invasion and a homecoming, aggressive and familiar all at once. I wanted to shove him away, to scream at him for assuming I wanted his touch after everything that happened. But my body remembered *before*, and melted into the familiarity of his touch, betraying my resolve. His lips moved against mine with a desperation that mirrored my own, pouring years of apology and longing into the gesture.

When he finally pulled back, he didn't go far. His forehead rested against mine, his breath mingling with mine, heavy and hot. "I'm sorry," he whispered hoarsely. "For everything. I had valid reasons I won't apologize for because, above everything else, I will always protect you, Apple."

"I never doubted you would." I was exasperated as well as hurt. "That's what you are. A protector to everyone you care about. But if you'd just explained it to me, we could have worked it out together."

"Not on something like this, honey. The men I had after me would have made the short remainder of your life a living hell just to torture me. It was worth risking my happiness to make sure you were as far away from those monsters as possible."

"And my happiness? What about my happiness?" He winced but shook his head. Before he could say anything, I continued in a whisper, "What is life without happiness, Deacon?"

"You'd have found happiness without me. You're young."

"I'm not too young to know what love is. I loved you, Deacon." My voice broke. "So much!"

"You still love me." So arrogant. He wasn't wrong.

"Maybe I do. But you lost any right you had to me when you told me you needed more than I could give you."

He nodded. "Agreed. I'm still taking you."

This time, when he kissed me, Deacon's touch was rough, desperate, filled with the anger and longing that had built between us over the last year and a half. I pushed against him, angry at myself for responding despite my better judgment and my bruised pride.

"Don't fight me, Apple," Deacon whispered between kisses. "I can't stay away from you any longer. You're mine. You always have been."

With that, he wrapped his arms around me and

lifted me. I couldn't stop my legs from going around his waist. I still gripped his shoulders with my hands instead of winding my arms around his neck, but I clung to him as though my life depended on it. Or like I never wanted to let him go.

The heat of the moment swirled around us, a tempest of unresolved feelings and unspoken words. Deacon carried me to the bedroom, setting me down on the bed with a gentleness that belied his earlier aggression. His eyes searched mine, as if looking for an answer. Or perhaps permission?

"I need you to understand something," he said, his voice rasping with emotion. "When I left, it wasn't because I didn't love you. It was because loving you too much could have killed you."

I stared at him, tears brimming in my eyes, anger mingling with the torrent of love. "You're so frustrating!"

Deacon lay down on top of me, his heavy weight pressing me into the mattress. "I know."

"I can't do this with you." I looked away from him, pushing at his shoulders. "Let me up."

"No."

"You don't get to say no to me, Deacon. Not about this." I bared my teeth at him. My lower body rocked against him without my permission. The hard ridge of his cock slid between my legs like it belonged there. I shuddered in pleasure I was afraid to let myself sample because I knew one taste would never be enough. Even now, with just his kisses and the delicious, heady feeling of his body pressed so intimately against mine, I wasn't sure I could deny myself the pleasure of fucking him. Because that demand was beating at me like hell wouldn't have it.

"You tell me right now you don't want my cock

buried so deep inside you you'll never be able to get it out, and I'll leave you. Tell me you don't dream about waking up in my arms. Tell me you don't love me, Apple."

I opened my mouth to tell him exactly that, but nothing came out. Probably because Deacon's expression had hardened, a warning about lying to him. Again a wave of frustration slammed into me. "Don't you dare get on that kick where you demand I not lie to you. How many times did you lie to me since that one perfect night we spent together?" The tears did come this time. "I thought you were giving me your property patch. That we'd end up back in our home, making love. I slept in your arms that night, believing that I had a lifetime of nights just like that one ahead of me. Then you just… left!" I shoved at him again. He lifted his body off to ease the pressure but didn't let me push him all the way off me.

"The only way I'm getting off you right now is if I'm hurting you. I never want to cause you pain unless it's to give you pleasure, but I'm not going anywhere. Never again."

My breath hitched as Deacon's words sank in, the raw need in his voice acting as a balm and a poison all at once. "You can't just decide for both of us. That's what got us in this situation to begin with. It's not fair to either of us."

"It's not about fair, Apple. It's about survival, yours and mine." His fingers traced the line of my jaw gently, a stark contrast to the intensity burning in his eyes. "Every minute away from you was hell. I knew if I was followed or we were seen together, they'd come after you harder than they were coming after me simply because I love you. Knowing what could happen…" He swallowed hard, looking away momentarily before locking eyes with me again. "I couldn't live with myself if anything happened to you. I stopped the immediate threat to you when I took out Illivitch. I've not met the next guy I'm going after so the danger to you isn't as bad. Besides, if you're here in the Grim Road compound, you're as safe as you could be anywhere. More so." He kissed me again, taking his time, sweeping his tongue into my mouth with infinite care. It wasn't until my body softened in his arms and I sighed in contentment that Deacon ended the kiss, nuzzling my cheek. My ear. My neck. "When Lemon called me and told me you'd been shot..." His big body trembled against mine, his breath catching. I felt the truth of it then. He'd been terrified, though Deacon wasn't a man who feared much. "I felt like my world was coming to an end. The thought that I'd never see you again brought me to my Goddamned knees. I knew there was no way I could not have you in my life."

"Deacon." I breathed his name like a prayer. And maybe it was. My most fervent prayer was that he'd come back to me and never leave. "Please don't promise me something else you can't or won't deliver. My heart --" My voice caught as tears trickled from the corner of my eyes down my temples. "I can't go through this again. It nearly broke me before."

"I swear to you on my life, Apple." Deacon shifted his weight to one arm and brought my hand to his chest. "On my Goddamned life. I will never leave you again, and I will always talk to you. From now on, we make decisions together."

I stared into his hazel eyes, searching for the truth. I wasn't sure I could find what I needed there, but I could see how much he believed what he was telling me. I suppose it came down to how much I wanted Deacon. Was I willing to risk hurting like that again if it meant I got an honest chance at making Deacon mine? Of me being his?

Decision made, I sighed, sliding my arms around Deacon's neck. "You hurt me, Deacon. So very badly." I held his gaze a couple seconds longer. "Don't do it again."

He nodded. "Never again. I swear you won't regret giving me another chance."

"I better not. It happens again, you'll have to deal with Lemon."

"Fully aware. Also the whole of Iron Tzars and likely Grim Road too."

"Just so long as there are no misunderstandings."

Deacon threaded his hands through my hair and held me still for his kiss again. I'd only ever kissed one other man besides Deacon and I hadn't even kissed Deacon for the last year and a half. Not sure it mattered though. I doubted if I'd ever be immune to Deacon's touch. At least, I never wanted to be. As one of his hands moved along my side to my hip, I relaxed beneath him, letting him touch me at will. I arched up so my breasts rubbed against his chest.

And just like that, I thought I might die if I couldn't have him right this second. I cried out against his lips and Deacon swallowed my scream. He urged my leg higher on his hip so he could rock against me, rubbing his cock between my legs over my pussy. My body jerked in reaction and Deacon gripped my ass through my thin, cotton shorts, squeezing and kneading almost reflexively.

Then he let out a deep sigh, pulling back to bury his face in my neck. "Christ, Apple. What the fuck am I gonna do with you?"

"What do you want to do with me?" I gazed up

at him, my eyes wide.

"I want to eat you up," he growled.

Chapter Seven
Deacon

Christ. I was so fucked. I definitely shouldn't have said I wanted to eat her up, but it was the truth. Every fiber of my being hummed with the need to have Apple, to claim her as mine in every way that mattered. It wasn't just physical, though God knew that part was overwhelming. It was deeper, carved into the very marrow of my bones.

"I mean it," I continued, my voice hoarse with raw emotion. "I want all of you, Apple. Every single piece. This time, I absolutely will not give you up. No matter what."

Every damn cell in my body screamed for her. The way she looked up at me, those big blue eyes made me feel like some kind of hero instead of the mess I really was. But God, she'd believed in me once, believed in us, and that made all the difference. I knew I had a long way to go before she trusted me again. I deserved her anger.

"We need to talk about this, Deacon." Her voice was rough with emotion. "Really talk. About everything. I'm not referring to your reasons for leaving. I'm talking about you leaving at all." She pushed me away just enough to see my face clearly but allowing me to still cover her delectable body with my own.

I loved our size difference. Always had. When I'd first found out how young she was, I'd had reservations about making her mine, but the longer I was around her, the more I learned how truly gentle and good she was, the more I craved her. If anything, the age and experience disparity sent a thrill through me. I wanted to be the man to corrupt little Apple, though, I had the feeling she'd give me a run for my money if she ever went all in with me.

"Yeah, baby. I know. I know," I grunted before leaning down to kiss her again. I couldn't help it. Any distance between us once I'd started this was completely unacceptable. "Let me take care of you, Apple. I swear I'll never leave you again."

She looked at me. I could see the indecision in her eyes. I also could tell she didn't believe me.

"Don't promise me things you can't deliver on, Deacon." She reached up and brushed my cheek with her cool palm. "I want you, but I don't expect a happily-ever-after."

"Tough. I'm never leaving you again, so you're stuck with me."

She didn't look convinced as she continued to pet my cheek as if for her own comfort. I knew I absorbed her touch like a hungry sponge.

The silence between us stretched, loaded with a million unspoken thoughts and raw emotions. I watched as Apple's eyes flickered with a painful kind of hope, tinged by the shadows of past disappointments. It was clear she was fighting a war within herself, trying to decide whether to guard her heart or surrender to what we both felt pulsating between us like a living thing.

As much as I wanted to believe my own words, to make them solid and real, doubts gnawed at me. Not doubts about Apple or if she was the woman I wanted. I knew unequivocally Apple was the woman I needed in my life. She was the bright spot in my life that made all the ugly bearable. Being without her for more than a year after seeing her nearly every day had me feeling stretched. Thin. Like my sanity was on the very edge. Apple soothed me in ways I had never appreciated. *Before.*

"I can't think about the future now, Deacon. Not now."

"I'll give you everything," I said, my voice fervent, desperate even. "Anything you want, anything you need from me. I'm always gonna be here, baby. I was wrong to leave you like I did."

"I understand you had things to do for the club. Iron Tzars needs good men like you. I get you were trying to take down a human trafficking ring and I'd never get in the way of your work. What hurt the most was the way you shut me out. It's like you saw me as a child instead of your woman."

"Apple..." I breathed out a sigh and buried my face in her neck. I wanted to deny she was right, but I couldn't. "I thought I knew what was best for you. I just wanted to keep you safe. Even from me."

"You'd never hurt me, Deacon. I know that. And I get you were trying to make sure no one could get to you through me. Not for yourself. But for me."

"Don't kid yourself, baby. I did it for me too. The thought of being the reason someone tried to hurt you was more than I could handle. It made me need to push you away, even at the expense of your own happiness. You're young. I hoped you'd get over me and move on." I frowned. "No. That's not true. The thought of you with another man ain't somethin' I can deal with either."

"What exactly were you hoping to accomplish?" That was my Apple. She was compassionate, intelligent, and no-nonsense when she needed to be. She also knew me well enough to know I was only telling half the truth.

"Christ." I scrubbed a hand over my face as I rolled off her to my back on the bed. I took her with me, though she was sprawled on top of me. "All I could think about was keeping you safe. Makin' sure none of that filth ever touched you."

"You can't control everything, Deacon. It touched me without anything to do with you. Calista and Olivia are my friends. I might not have met them if I hadn't come to be with Lemon." She sighed, then laid her head on my shoulder. Her legs straddled my hips and it was all I could do not to raise my hips to find contact with her sweet cunt. Even if it was through her shorts. "I learned to live without you. Here. In this place. Now, you invaded my hiding place. I pushed my way through losing you once. I'm not doing it again. So, if you're not sure or if you plan on going off to fight a war or take down a small country, or go fight the cartel over their skin trade, I want you to leave. Now. If you don't, I'm not ashamed to pull my sister's rank and get her to kick you out."

"Ain't goin' nowhere ever again unless you're with me. That means I request to patch in with Grim Road, then that's what I do."

She didn't move for a long while. Her head on my shoulder, she snuggled her face against my neck and lay there. In the years I'd spent with Apple in the Iron Tzars MC compound, I'd cuddled with her plenty. Even after I'd left. When I did manage to come home, I spent time with her watching a movie on the couch with her in my arms under a blanket. Sure, my hands had drifted. Hers had too. But even those wonderful touches paled in comparison with how it felt to have Apple in my arms right now.

"I don't know if I trust you with my heart, Deacon. I'm not sure I'll ever get there. But I want to give you my body. At least, for now. I can't promise anything after tonight, though. I just know I'll regret it if I don't take this time with you. After that, we can go about our business and reevaluate our expectations for each other."

"I'll be what you need. From here on out. Ain't never gonna be parted from you again. We're a team."

She raised herself and rested on the arm she braced on my chest. "We'll see. For now, I want to live in the moment." Leaning in to brush her lips over mine, she whispered, "Fuck me, Deacon. I want to know what it's like to have you inside me."

Christ! Her words were a siren's song, calling a helpless mortal to the sea to be devoured. And, Goddamn, if I didn't go willingly. I'd take whatever she offered and beg her for more if it meant I got to stay with her for the rest of my life.

Rolling over so that she was beneath me, I trapped her gaze with mine, intensity flaring between us like a live wire. "You sure about this?" I asked, voice a gravelly rumble, my eyes searching hers for any hint of hesitation. "Much as I want you, I want you to want me too."

Her fingers traced the tattoo on my chest just beneath the collar of my T-shirt, a slight tremor in her touch betraying her nerves. But when she spoke, her voice was steady. "I've never been more sure of anything in my life."

I kissed her then, a kiss that spoke of raw hunger and years of pent-up longing. My hands roamed over her, needing to memorize every curve of her lithe form. I rocked my hips from side to side, settling myself in the cradle of her body.

Her fingers tugged up my shirt to find skin. The second her palms settled on my skin, she let out a contented sigh. Like she'd been waiting to touch me forever and finally got her wish. She'd had her hands on my bare chest before, but nothing like this. She slid her palms from my sides around to my back -- still under my shirt -- only to dig her nails into my flesh. God! It felt so fucking right!

Apple's breath hitched, her nails dragged along my skin, sending shivers down my spine. I deepened the kiss, and our breathing became erratic as the space between us grew charged with electricity. Her legs wrapped around my lower back, pulling me closer, urging me to erase all the empty spaces that had kept us apart for too long.

Kissing Apple was everything. It had always been my most fervent dream, especially when I was away from her, but this time... This was different. This wasn't a woman experimenting with a would-be lover. This was a woman who knew what she wanted and was determined to take it.

Breaking the kiss, I looked into her eyes, dark with desire and something deeper, something like a dare. "Tell me what you want," I whispered against her lips, needing to hear her say it again, needing to make this moment perfect for her as well as making sure it was real and not some kind of hallucination.

Her eyes locked onto mine, fierce and unyielding. "I told you, Deacon. I want you to fuck me. Make it good." I tilted my head at her, knowing there was more she wanted to say but that she was reluctant to say it. She sucked in a deep breath, then let it out. "If this is the only time I get to have you, I want it to be good." She moved one hand to my face, gripping my beard hard. "Show me what I've been missing."

"Tell me, Apple. You been with anyone besides me? Kissed another man?"

She raised an eyebrow, not letting go of me, but loosening her grip on my beard. She stroked her fingers through it almost reverently. Her expression told another story, however. Her eyes flashed with anger and pain. "And if I have? Isn't that what you told me to do? To find a guy I could be happy with?"

I couldn't help the surge of jealousy. Judging by the smirk on her face, she noticed it too. "Apple..."

She shrugged. "That's none of your business."

"So long as you don't do it again." Yeah, that popped out before I could censor myself.

"Oh, really?" Her eyes widened and she raised a disbelieving eyebrow at me. "You telling me you ain't been with another woman? It's been more than four years since we met. You told me before you hadn't been with a woman since we committed to each other. You don't expect me to believe you've not fucked another woman in all that time. Especially after you broke up with me."

"You don't have to believe it, Apple. But I haven't. A man can get off without having pussy."

"So? You got someone to suck you off. Or fucked her ass. Or maybe you found a man?" Again, she shrugged. "Makes no difference to me. We're not committed anymore. Haven't been since you came back to Iron Tzars."

I growled, knowing she was right but unable to keep the jealousy at bay. "Pushing you away was necessary, Apple. And believe what you want. But I've not touched or been touched by anyone in a sexual manner since the last time I kissed you."

"Not sure I believe that, but whatever." She turned away but her legs tightened around my waist, like she wanted me to leave but wasn't fully committed to the idea.

"You don't have to believe me, baby. Just know that it's you for me. Always has been."

"You said I was too young for you."

"I was trying to push you away."

Now, she looked angry. "Why, Deacon? Why not let me make my own decision?"

"Because, I needed you safe and you're too stubborn and loyal to have left when I told you to. Especially after me being gone for so long." I buried my face in her neck again, loving the scent of her. Loving the closeness even if it did feel like there was still an invisible barrier between us now.

"Are you gonna fuck me or not? Because you're really killing the mood now."

I thrust my hips at her, letting the ridge of my cock ride over her clit. I knew I'd hit the right spot because her breath hitched and her eyes widened just a fraction. She shifted beneath me before stilling as if realizing what she'd just done. "Killin' the mood? I don't think so. I think you want me just as much as I want you."

"Don't mean anything." She stuck up her chin, a stubborn gesture if ever I saw one. "I've wanted you to fuck me for a long time. Just this time, I'll know not to let my heart get involved."

Yeah. Challenge accepted.

Chapter Eight

Apple

I was in trouble. The look in Deacon's eyes said he was a man on a mission. I was terribly afraid that mission was to get me to give him something I didn't want to. My heart.

But I couldn't worry about that right now. The second Deacon lowered his lips to mine again, I knew he was out for blood. He swept inside my mouth like a conquering hero -- or villain -- and made me forget about anything other than hanging on and accepting his dominance. Because only he held the key to the pleasure I knew lay just beyond my reach.

Just when I knew I'd never be able to breathe without his lips on mine, Deacon pushed off me to sit back on his heels, my legs draped over his thighs. He watched me intently as he whipped off his shirt to reveal his ripped, tattooed body. No matter how many times I'd watched him working out shirtless, or gone swimming with him, looking at his rugged body always brought a rush of pleasure.

"Take it off, baby. I want your top and bra off."

It took his words a moment to kick in from my brain to my body, but the second I processed his gruff demand, I scrambled to comply. Which meant I was proving him right to not like our age difference. There was no way I could ever be the woman he expected me to be. I mean, I'd learn, but that was the problem. Deacon had to be willing to teach me. If he wasn't, this was already doomed. Which I would not think about! I'd decided I was taking what he offered and living in the moment, so that's what I was going to do.

I refused to look at his face, to see any kind of displeasure and reached for him once I'd tossed the offending garments over the side of the bed. Instead, I kept my gaze firmly on his chest. Hopefully, he'd think I was mesmerized by his body -- which wouldn't exactly be off the mark -- and not question me.

"Christ," he bit out. "Get your fuckin' shorts off too."

I wiggled my shorts over my hips and off my ass, lifting my legs for Deacon to tug them down -- panties and all. He tossed them to the floor, then gripped my thighs and pulled my lower body up with a sharp tug. All I could do was gasp in a breath before letting it out on a scream as his mouth went straight to my pussy and *sucked*.

My body arched as Deacon's rough tongue found my clit, licking and swirling around the bundle of nerves with purpose. I reveled in every single sensation, from his unshaven jaw rasping against my vulnerable skin to the feather-light touches of his breath on my folds. Every so often, he licked up along the length of my slit, teasing my clit as it throbbed for him, plumping it with his actions. A guttural groan rumbled in his chest as he suckled on me, a low growling noise that came from deep within him, full of need and desire. His fingers on my legs squeezed tighter, pulling them farther apart until I was fully exposed to his clever mouth, teeth, and tongue. How long had I dreamt about being in this exact position? Too long. Too fucking long.

I tried to push myself farther into his mouth, to rub my clit over his beard but it wasn't enough. I needed more friction! My hips bucked up and down, begging for penetration as he lapped at my sex. My nails dug into the sheets, the textured cotton soft against my palms. I threw my head back, keeping myself from pleading with him to fuck me as he had promised. To take what he was denying himself so far.

"God! Sweet God!"

"God has very little to do with this, baby." Deacon looked down at me from between my legs. My weight rested on my shoulders while my knees hooked over his shoulders. If there was a twinge from my injury, I didn't mind. Just meant I was alive and in the arms of the man I loved with all my heart. I thrust my hips up and down, needing more. Needing what he was denying us both.

"Why are you waiting?" The question was ripped from me against my will. I wanted all he had to give me, but I wasn't prepared to beg him. Definitely not this fast. If there was any doubt I'd come to him inexperienced, this was it. I needed to keep my mouth shut. Let him do what he wanted and be happy. Maybe then I could manage to prove I could be what he needed. I'd follow his lead without hesitation and maybe I could convince him I just really enjoyed sex and hope he ignored the possibility I'd come to him a virgin. That was the last thing I wanted him to know.

"Because I've waited for this moment for fuckin' ever. The second I get inside you, it's fuckin' over because I will come so fuckin' hard I'll never recover."

I had to study him to determine if he was telling the truth. Which was difficult given the fact he was driving me fucking crazy with his mouth on my pussy. I wanted to believe him, but I just didn't have enough experience to know for sure. He was sweating, and I thought his hands shook where he held my thighs, but I was trembling so much I couldn't be sure.

Deacon's hands roamed over my thighs and ass cheeks possessively, claiming every inch of my skin he touched. Then one hand slid down my torso to cup and squeeze one breast. I cried out at the unexpected pleasure.

"So gentle and dainty," he murmured. "Exquisite. Never knew a woman could be so fierce yet so delicate."

"I'm not delicate." The protest came out breathy so I wasn't sure if he believed me.

Deacon's eyes darkened further at my protest, and he pulled away from my aching pussy, giving it one last long lick with his tongue before he let my legs go. He moved from the bed and kicked off his shoes. Stripping off his jeans and boxers, he stepped out of them. He pulled his wallet out of his back pocket and taking out a condom before tossing the condom packet to the bed and his clothing and wallet onto a nearby chair. His socks soon followed. His impressive cock bobbed before him, ready to be sheathed in the warmth of my pussy. It was thick and veiny, heavily flushed with pre-cum glistening at the tip. He picked up the condom packet again, tearing it open and rolling it on with practiced ease, never taking his eyes off mine.

"This is your last chance, Apple. You sure you're ready?"

"I've been ready a long time, Deacon." My voice was a mere thread of sound as I stared at his cock. I wanted it with greedy abandon. Wanted him. Deacon.

He growled low in his throat, a sound that made my stomach flip with excitement. He crawled back on top of me, rubbing my body with his until he settled back in the cradle of my thighs. He gripped my hips firmly and guided his cock to my entrance, teasing me by pushing forward slightly before pulling back again. His tortured expression was both arousing and terrifying, a heady combination that had me writhing under his touch.

"Please..." I whimpered before I could quell the

sound. Deacon pushed forward once more, breaching my tight pussy with one slow thrust. There was a jolt of pain mixed with pleasure, shooting through me like fireworks in the sky. I tried not to wince because I knew he'd know I'd never been with a man if I didn't. I had to make it through this without embarrassing myself. If this was the only time I ever got to be with Deacon, I wanted it to be perfect. Though, I had to admit, if he kept playing my body like he'd been doing, it might be worth the embarrassment.

"Fuck!" Deacon groaned, grabbing onto my hips tighter as he began to move in and out of me, each stroke deeper than the last. The friction was exquisite, but I needed more -- I needed him to take control completely.

"Please," I begged again, arching up into him as he hit something deep inside of me that sent sparks shooting through my core. He caught me by the waist and slammed into me hard then, claiming me completely with each rough thrust.

Deacon lay fully on top of me, his arms wrapped around me, his hips moving harder and harder as he fucked me like he needed to. My mind felt like it was fracturing. The pleasure was overwhelming and numbing at the same time. It was as if I was on some kind of sensory overload, my body refusing to process anything more.

"Fuck... fuck!" Deacon growled as he looked down into my face. I was sure I just stared at him in awe. How could a man bring so much pleasure to one woman? It was in that moment that I understood exactly what he'd meant when he said I was too damned young for him. No doubt a woman older and more experienced in sex would know what to do in this situation. She could bring him as much pleasure as he brought her and all I could do was lie there while he took me.

That last thought pushed me over the edge of something vast and deep. I'd made myself come before, but it was never like this. Never so all-consuming and wild. I gave a startled cry before the wave crashed over me like a raging torrent.

Deacon felt the change in my body, the way my muscles tightened around him, and he let out a deep, satisfying groan. His thrusts became even more determined, pushing us both toward something cataclysmic. I clung to him, my nails digging into his back, marking him as intensely as he marked me.

As the wave of my climax began to ebb, Deacon's movements grew more desperate, more primal. His face was contorted with concentration and pleasure, a sight that only fueled my desire further. Sweat dripped from his face to mine and I reveled in it. The room echoed with the sound of our bodies slamming together, a rhythm that wrote its own carnal music in the air. Then he bowed his back, his face turned to the ceiling. With a lingering bellow, Deacon came. His cock pulsed inside me triggering another orgasm for me. I cried out again as I clung to him, my only anchor in the storm he'd created within me.

Deacon collapsed on top of me, his movements stilled as my body shuddered beneath him, his eyes searching my face for something I couldn't name. His breath was as ragged as my own, his forehead creased with a mix of concern and unstoppable desire. He must have seen the bliss in my expression, because his lips twisted into a satisfied grin before he rested fully on top of me, his cock still buried snugly inside my pussy.

"Apple," he whispered against the skin of my neck, his voice rough with emotion. He kissed my jaw.

My cheek. My mouth. His words vibrated through me, creating its own pleasure. "You're incredible."

I wrapped my legs tighter around him, not wanting this interlude to end. I wanted more. I wanted to do this all night. Maybe then I'd get my fill of this incredible man. The man I was completely head over heels in love with.

Chapter Nine

Deacon

The next two weeks were equal parts heaven and hell. Heaven because I spent every waking moment in Apple's presence. Well, when she allowed it. Hell because she took every opportunity to slip away from me which meant I had to actively hunt her down. She'd never run from me. *Before.*

Yeah. That fucking word. Before. I hated it. It represented the absolute worst time in my life and how the fallout had affected Apple no matter how much I'd intended to protect her. I thought pushing her away as I did had hurt her worse than the gunshot wound. I knew she loved me, but I suppose I hadn't realized just how much she was invested in me.

Until she wasn't.

Now, I sat under a big tree next to the clubhouse, I watched her and all the old ladies of the club as they talked and drank peach Crown Royal. I mean, it was still whisky. Right? Occasionally, one or more of them would glance in my direction, but not Apple. She ignored me as thoroughly as a princess ignoring the pig farmer peasant.

Evelyn, Knox's woman, kept narrowing her eyes at me. Like she wanted to carve out my liver. Olivia would occasionally cast me furtive glances so it was hard to know how she felt. I was pretty sure she hated me too, but also knew I was the man who'd make sure her stepfather was completely out of her life forever. Bear's woman, Cecilia, was friendly enough, but there was no doubt she was solidly in Apple's corner no matter what. So if Apple decided she hated me, Cecilia would follow suit.

What puzzled me was how Lemon and Venus

reacted. Lemon seemed to be on my side, pushing Apple toward me instead of pushing me away from her sister. Venus followed Lemon's lead. Or maybe it was the other way around. I'd seen the two women conversing several times since I'd come here. Always, they were either looking at me or Apple.

At first, I thought Lemon didn't want me with her sister, but that didn't really make sense because she was the one who'd told me Apple had been shot in the first place. She told me Apple needed me and to drop what I was doing and get my ass to Riviera Beach. So, I wasn't sure if Lemon was getting advice from Venus or Venus was telling her she was making a colossal mistake pushing me and her sister together again.

Finally, Apple looked my way. I didn't dare move or take my gaze from hers. Every time I managed to catch her attention outside of my bedroom, there was a split second of vulnerability in her expression before it hardened and she rolled her eyes, dismissing me. *Princess to peasant.*

This time, she held my gaze for several seconds before ducking her head and leaving the group. And yeah, every single one of the women looked my way. I sighed. Lucky me.

"You know," a voice behind me started. I turned to find Venus leaning a shoulder against the tree. Her other hand rested on her hip. As usual, she was in pink from head to toe. "She loves you."

I turned back to watch Apple as she walked to her house just across the path next to the women's favorite meeting spot on the property. "She's afraid I'll hurt her again." I shrugged. "I don't blame her."

"You did do number on her before she came here." Venus's light Russian accent always felt just as eerie as the rest of her. She was pleasant enough, but

I'd been told she'd been an assassin before joining Salvation's Bane MC a long time ago. Her sister, Millie, was just as deadly and dangerous as Venus, and Thorn, the president of Bane, considered her the deadliest member of his club.

"I thought it was the only way to keep her safe." Listening to myself after everything that had happened both to me and Apple since I'd left, my excuse sounded pretty damned hollow.

"And now?" Christ. Even the woman's elegant eyebrows were fucking pink. She raised one at me in question now.

I sighed, scrubbing a hand over my face several times. "I may have overreacted."

"Why would you overreact?"

"I think both you and Lemon know I love Apple. I was trying to protect her by sending her to a place where no one could find her."

"You know Iron Tzars could have protected her just as well."

"I wasn't willing to take the chance. Besides, Lemon is the better warrior. Danica loves her sister, but Lemon is a protector through and through. I knew the safest place for Apple was with her twin."

Venus nodded, giving me a slight smile. "Very true. You could have used delicate touch, and she might have gone in direction you wanted. Instead, you made her run. From you."

"Yeah. Apple should always run toward me. Not away."

"What will you do about it?"

I stood then, dusting off my backside, then brushing my hands together. "I'll let you know when I figure it out, but I'm sure groveling will be involved."

"You're gonna have an uphill battle, Deacon."

Lemon approached us, worry on her face as she glanced in the direction her sister had gone. "Why did you have to humiliate her like you did? Huh?" She took a couple of steps toward me and kicked me right in the crotch. I didn't see it coming, though I should have. Lemon might want me and Apple together, but she'd never hesitate to give me what she owed me.

"Christ, Lemon!"

"You think she hurt less than that? If so, you can hit me back."

I looked up at her from where I'd fallen to my knees on the ground. "Never said I didn't hurt her." My voice was strained, and I knew I grimaced in pain. "I intended to hurt her and I did."

"Yeah, ya did." Lemon shook her head, giving me a look that said she was sorry for me, but I was still going to have to die. "You know I have to kick your ass for that. Right?"

"Yeah, Lemon." I grunted as I got carefully to my feet. My balls were singing and I wasn't sure I could stand, let alone walk. But I was going after Apple. "I know. But can we do that later? I don't really have time right now."

Venus let out a snort, then chuckled. Her contralto voice was deep and throaty. "Those two belong together."

"It's the only reason he gets to live." Lemon jerked her head in Apple's direction. "I really thought you'd have her locked down by now, Deacon. I was in your corner. You're makin' me look bad."

"She wants me, but she's afraid to let me get too close to her."

"Do you blame her?" Lemon asked.

I faced her then, looking into her eyes so she could see the truth. "No. I don't blame her. She has every right to not trust me. I did this to protect her. After she got hurt, when you told me she needed me, I knew I could never leave her again. Where she goes, I go."

"You better keep your promise this time, Deacon. You're getting a second chance. Don't make me regret giving it to you."

Not wanting to let Apple out of my sight for long, I stumbled in her direction, groaning as my balls protested the movement.

She was just shutting the door to her home when I reached the small yard. If she saw or heard me, she gave no indication. The door slamming harder than necessary told me all I needed to know about if she'd want me there or not.

I climbed the two steps to the front porch and knocked on the door. "Apple? It's me."

"Sorry, Deacon. We'll have to get together tomorrow. I've got a date with Falcon tonight," she called to me from behind the door, not bothering to open it. I knew she was trying to get a dig at me. She'd done it several times since we'd had sex. Just little digs, telling me to get lost or that she'd gotten what she wanted from me. I could go now. This was the first time she'd actually named a man from Grim Road, though.

"Apple. Open the door."

"Is Falcon with you? If so, he's early."

"Apple. Open the fuckin' door."

The door opened, Apple draping a towel over her front like she'd been in the process of changing clothes. An irritated look was on her face as she looked past me. Looking for Falcon?

"If he shows up here, I'll kill the son of a bitch." I bared my teeth at her.

Apple lifted her chin. "No you won't. He's my choice."

"*I'm* your choice, Apple."

"Just because I fucked you doesn't mean I want a relationship. I scratched an itch. Nothing more."

Chapter Ten

Deacon

"*Scratched an itch?*" This was my penance. To hear her reduce the best sexual experience of my life to nothing more than a romp in the hay. And wasn't it supposed to be the man doing that? Why was everything with Apple and Lemon always backward?

"Yeah. I mean, I had a great time and everything, but I only wanted the one time. To see what it was like." Her eyes widened. "I mean, with you. I wanted to see what it was like with you." She shrugged and play-punched my shoulder. "Not bad, slugger."

I heard a bike headed down the path toward us and wrapped my arm around Apple as it pulled into her drive. Fucking Falcon. The other man shut off his bike and climbed off. I immediately stepped in front of Apple. If Falcon saw her naked, I'd have to pluck out his eyeballs.

"Huh." He looked from me to Apple and back. "We still on, sweetheart?" Apple tried to step around me but that was happening over my dead body. I mirrored her move and kept Apple out of Falcon's direct line of sight as much as possible.

"Yes," she said at the same time I said, "No."

"Right. Deacon, I think maybe you better leave." Falcon was all business, but I saw his lips twitch in amusement.

"And I think you better mind your own damned business. *You* fuckin' leave."

"Not happening, bro. Not unless Apple says so."

"She says so," I spat out.

Falcon, the fucker, just grinned. "Her mouth ain't movin'. Ain't hearin' her say nothin'."

"Well, she does. Now, get the fuck on. She's

taken."

"She's not taken!" Apple tried to shove away from me, but I wasn't having that.

"Nothing comes between us, Apple," I growled, looking back at her. "Nothing. Especially not that little pissant."

Falcon put his hands on his hips as he stood there, scowling at me. "I thought we shared a moment back when you took care of Illivitch, bro. Where's the love?"

"Kiss my ass, Pigeon Nuts."

Falcon immediately stiffened, his arms dropping to his sides and curling into fists. "Lemon. That little bitch. She told you, didn't she." It wasn't a question and I couldn't deny it. "I'm goin' to Rocket over this. He needs to beat her ass but good!" he muttered to himself as he climbed back on his bike. "Pigeon Nuts. Woman's a fuckin' menace."

Once Falcon left, I shut and locked the door before turning back to Apple. She still held the towel to her front and now I was wondering if she was naked or if she had underwear on. Didn't see any straps at her shoulders, but I suppose any bra she had on could be strapless.

I cleared my throat, trying to ignore the way my cock was at full attention now. "Why have you been avoiding me?"

She gave a delicate snort. "I've not been avoiding you. I'm just done with you. You served your purpose. Now I'm moving on."

"Right. So you could see what it was like to fuck me."

She curled a finger over her lips like she was really thinking about my words and nodded. "Yep. Sounds about right." Little brat. So much like her sister. She was trying to protect herself and punish me some more. I knew that. Still hurt, but I didn't deserve anything less.

"Yeah?" I stalked her across the small space separating us. When she didn't back down or retreat even an inch, I wanted to smile, to let her know I was proud of her for not being intimidated by me even though I could see little wisps of her hair quivering. She was trembling. Maybe not in fear in the conventional sense, but she was definitely afraid of me. Probably that I'd break her heart again. "Well, maybe I'm not done with you."

I reached for her slowly. When she didn't try to get free, I pulled her against me, wrapping my arms around her in an embrace. Her towel and my clothes were the only things between us, and it felt damned good.

She didn't resist but didn't return the affection either. Just stiffened in my arms. This close, with my body surrounding hers, I could feel Apple shaking. Fine tremors racked her and she held her breath, letting it out slowly only to quickly suck in another one. I thought she might be fighting off tears. When I pulled back to look down at her, searching her face for any signs of what she was thinking, I saw she hadn't been as successful at holding back the offending drops as she might have liked.

"I really do hate you," she whispered as tears continued to leak from her eyes and drip down her cheeks.

"I know, baby. I deserve it too. But I'm going to make you a promise right here. Right now." I cupped her face with my palms, swiping under her eyes with my thumbs. "I want you to listen to me. Really listen." When she continued to stare up at me with her big blue eyes glistening I nearly groaned in defeat. This woman *owned me*! "I'm never leaving you again. Understand?"

"You said that before," she whispered, shaking her head. "How am I supposed to believe you?"

"Faith, baby. Give me your faith and I swear to you, I'll never hurt you again."

She studied me for a long time. So long I was tempted to continue arguing my case. It wouldn't be a good idea, which was the only way I held my tongue and just let her come to her own conclusions. I stroked her cheek with small movements of my thumb. It was a compulsion I couldn't ignore. Any time she was near, I needed to touch her and knew I always would.

Then she did something I didn't expect. Her expression crumbled and she threw herself into my arms, wrapping her arms and legs around me. "You hurt me so bad, Deacon. I was so lost. I tried to find someone else. I asked Falcon to come here because I wanted to hurt you as bad as you hurt me."

"I know, baby. You had every right to lash out. What I did was inexcusable. I don't expect you to forgive me. I just want another chance to prove to you I can be the protector you need."

She pushed back then, not unwrapping her legs from my waist, just leaned back so she could really see me. "I don't need a protector, Deacon. I have all kinds of people here willing to protect me, and they'd do a brilliant job of it. I need a man who loves me. Like Rocket loves Lemon. I want what they have together."

"Well, I ain't lettin' you be an officer in the club so don't even ask."

She gave me an exasperated look. "Do you even have that kind of pull with Iron Tzars? How long have you even been a patched member?"

I had to chuckle. My girl was hurting, still crying, and she was still giving me shit.

"Christ, I love you, Applejack." The words just slipped out, but they felt right. Like I'd been waiting all my life to tell her that again. I had the feeling every single time I told her I loved her it would always feel like that. This woman was my *one*. No one else would ever do for me. "I have from the first day I met you." I grinned down at her shell-shocked expression. "Shoulda known then I needed to treat you differently than anyone else in my life. You're not a woman to sit by and watch while her man takes care of business. Just like your sister. Only... softer."

I expected her to scowl and tell me she was exactly like her sister and fuck me for saying she wasn't or something similar, but she just gave me a sheepish grin. "Lemon's always been the warrior. I'm the nurturer. I like taking care of people."

"I know, baby. It's part of why I wanted to protect you. Even from myself. If anything had happened to you because of me, I'd never forgive myself. I tried to keep you safe by making sure you were sent away somewhere no one would find you, but you got hurt anyway."

"And you came the second Lemon called you. I've been trying to hold on to my anger because of what you said that day, but the truth is, Lemon would have done the same thing for me. No matter how much it hurt. She might not have taken it as far as you did, but she'd have sent me wherever she thought I'd be the safest. And it kind of hurts to admit everyone in my life thinks I'm not strong enough to fight my own battles or to have their backs when they need it." She turned away as she said that last bit.

"Honey, it's not that we don't think you're

strong enough. You're as much a warrior as anyone here. You don't take shit and you're not afraid to give as good as you get. But that's not your nature. Me? Lemon? Everyone who knows you. We want to keep that part of you safe and encourage those tender feelings in you." I smiled at her before leaning in to brush my lips against hers briefly. "The truth is, we need people like you to keep us grounded. To remind us why we do what we do. Otherwise, the killin' we have to do would suck out our souls eventually."

She blinked up at me. "That might be the sweetest thing anyone's ever said to me."

That got a chuckle from me. "Well, it's the truth, baby. You are the heart and soul of everyone around you."

She leaned into my chest again, her tears wetting my shirt, but this time they seemed less bitter. "I just need you to promise me, Deacon. No more secrets, no more trying to shield me by pushing me away. If we're doing this... if we're really doing this, it's got to be together. All in, side by side."

I nodded, pressing my forehead against hers. "No more secrets," I confirmed. "Everything out in the open, even the ugly parts. Even the dangerous bits."

"That's all I ever wanted." Apple's eyes filled with tears again, but this time they sparkled with a different emotion -- hope, maybe even forgiveness. "You're still an asshole, though." She gave me a disgruntled look before pressing her lips to mine in a sweet kiss.

"Yeah, baby. Got that. Lemon made it known too."

She tilted her head. "Yeah? What'd she say?"

"Oh, it wasn't so much what she said as what she did. My balls hurt so bad I'm surprised I can walk straight."

Apple gave me a brilliant smile. "Good. That means I don't have to." Her smile faded then and she took on a serious mien. "I mean it, Deacon. If we do this, if we really try again, it can't be like before. You can't just decide things for me -- no matter how good your intentions are."

I nodded, understanding the weight of her words. "I know. And I swear to you I won't repeat the same mistakes. We'll make decisions together this time." It was a promise I intended to keep, a lesson I had learned the hard way. "I'm not going to lose you because I'm stupid, Apple."

She gave a delicate snort. And, really, it was just too cute for words. Finally, I could see my Apple peeking out from the fort she'd built around her emotions, and I wanted to thump my chest and howl with jubilation. "You're a guy, Deacon. It's an unspoken truth that you're gonna do stupid shit."

That made me bark out an unexpected laugh. "Yeah, baby. I can't deny that. Pesky Y chromosome."

"Exactly. Does something to muddle the mind."

And just like that, the weight of the world lifted just a little from my shoulders. My knees went weak, and I had to back up a couple steps to the sofa so I could collapse, still holding Apple tightly in my arms.

I buried my face in her neck, inhaling her sweet fragrance. "Fuckin' wildflowers and honey," I muttered against her skin.

"What?"

"Your smell. Wildflowers and honey."

She gave me a shy smile. "You like the way I smell?"

"I love every fuckin' thing about you, Apple."

She rested her head on my shoulder, and I felt

her relax in a way she hadn't in a long time. Not even after we'd made love. Her body was no longer tense with the burden of unspoken words and pent-up frustrations. Instead, there was a softness, an easing of the sharp edges that had defined our recent encounters. "I love you too, Deacon."

"You never made it a secret. You were all in with me from the very first. I was too. Just had trouble showing it. First because you were fuckin' sixteen. Then because of all the shit I had to do."

"Yeah, well, you can't say you weren't warned I was trouble. The signs were there."

I grinned. "Yeah. Trouble with a capital T-R-O-U-B-L-E."

Apple pulled back slightly, the glint of determination returning to her gaze. "Then we start fresh. *Tabula rasa.*"

I frowned. "What does that mean?"

"It's Latin for 'blank slate'."

"I like the sound of that."

"Just know that, if you do this again, if you break my heart like you did, Lemon won't have to kill you. I'll do it myself."

"I hear you, baby. Loud and clear."

"Good. Now. I think we should celebrate." She gave me a big, bright smile that had me melting, putty in her hands.

"Whatever you want. Name it and it's yours."

She leaned in to whisper in my ear. "I want to suck your cock. Then, when you can't hold back anymore, I want you to put me on my hands and knees, mount me from behind, and fuck the shit outta me."

And just like that, my cock and balls were feeling much fucking better. There was still an ache there, but it was no match for the raging hard-on her words conjured. I was also acutely aware her towel had slipped precariously, and she didn't seem to give a flying fuck.

"I think I can manage that. Gonna throw eatin' your pussy like a starvin' man in there in the middle, though. Been dreamin' about it."

"Well, if you insist. I'll sacrifice to give you what you want."

I threaded my fingers through her hair, chuckling as I brought her down for a hard kiss. She opened beautifully, letting me taste her. Her delicate tongue whispered over mine, following where I led us.

Our kiss deepened, a whirlwind of need and promise swirling between us, binding us tighter together than any vow spoken aloud could. As our mouths moved in sync, I could feel every past mistake washing away under the current of our renewed dedication and passion to each other.

Apple pulled away slightly, breathless, her eyes sparkling with a cocktail of desire and mischief. "To the bedroom?" she murmured, a playful challenge in her tone as she dropped the towel to the floor.

"Lead the way," I said with a grin. I was pretty sure there was drool at the corner of my mouth, because a naked Apple was too much to resist. If we didn't get to the bedroom soon, I knew I'd take her right there in the living room. I released her only long enough to grab her hand and follow her to our sanctuary.

The bedroom was dimly lit by the afternoon light filtering through gauzy curtains. Apple hadn't filled her bedroom with frilly female things. It was almost stark compared to what I'd seen in our little house at the Iron Tzars compound. Kind of like she didn't expect to be here long. I had to wonder if she wanted to come back to the Tzars. I knew Danica missed her. She also blamed me for Apple leaving and I wasn't sure forgiveness would come as easily to Dani as it had to Apple and Lemon.

At the bed, she turned and tugged off my shirt, so I undid my jeans. The more clothes I shed, the more urgent we both became. Apple's delicate, blonde brows knit together in concentration as she took in my torso. She reached out with one small hand and laid it over my heart before looking up at me.

"I'm yours and you're mine. Right?"

"From now on, baby. Hell, I've been yours since the day we met."

"I have a confession to make, then," she said distractedly as she traced a tattoo swirling over my pec. I wasn't one to man-groom or whatever. I had a hairy chest and made no apology. But I knew the tattoo she traced. I was surprised she hadn't noticed it the first time we'd made love.

"What is it, baby?"

Her brows knit together again as she studied the tatt. Then she smoothed her trembling hand over the mark. "When did you get this?" She didn't look up at me but continued to stare at my tattoo.

I covered her hand with my larger one. "The day you left Indiana." The tattoo was her name in ivy vines woven delicately around an apple blossom. "I had your name inked over my heart because wherever you go, my heart goes with you."

Her chin quivered, then to my surprise, she slapped at my chest, giving me a deep scowl. "When the fuck did you get to be such a romantic? I'm telling everyone at Iron Tzars. Your reputation will be ruined. You'll never get to be an officer." She gave me a pitying look. "Face it. Your life's gonna be ruined now." But tears started to drip from her eyes again, and she batted them away. "That's so sweet it's giving me a migraine *and* making my teeth rot."

I couldn't help but chuckle. "Well, when we get back to the Tzars, you know you've gotta get your own ink."

She froze. "Wait. Was that why you sent me away? You wouldn't give me a property cut, but you also didn't have me inked. I'd have done it, Deacon. I *want* to!"

"No, honey. That's not why I wanted you to go away. You know as well as I do, the men left in Iron Tzars would defend any woman in our compound to the death. Inked or not. It's still our way, but you and Lemon grew on everyone. Besides, you're Danica's sisters. That makes you family."

"I want your ink, Deacon." She gave me a fierce look. "And your property cut. That's nonnegotiable."

I grinned at her enthusiastic response. "You will, baby. I have your cut with me, and we'll get you inked the second we can."

"Good." She gave a firm nod. I could still see she was unsure. Probably would be until both those things happened, and I claimed her in front of the club. Well. That would start here. I'd do what I could, give her my cut, and make sure I was loud and proud about her being mine. The men in Grim Road knew I wanted her, but I hadn't had the chance to really stake a good, proper claim. Dragging her up to my room after meeting with Rocket and his officers had been a good start, but not nearly enough.

Chapter Eleven
Deacon

My phone buzzed where it lay in my jeans pocket on the floor, but I ignored it. I was not starting this second chance I'd been given by making that mistake. Instead, I pulled Apple into my arms and kissed her again.

The feel of her tits mashed against my chest was exquisite. She rubbed herself back and forth slightly, as if unsure what she was feeling, then she shuddered as she moaned in pleasure.

"Christ, Deacon! Your chest hair over my nipples…"

"Yeah? You like that?" I nibbled at her earlobe. "'Cause I bet my beard scrapin' those pouty nipples would feel just as good." She let out a startled cry and her whole body stiffened and she broke out into a full body sweat. "You like me talkin' dirty to you?"

"I love everything you do to me, Deacon. Since the very first time you ever held my hand." She sounded so young and sweet. Innocent.

Her responses were enthusiastic, always meeting my passion with a fire that only she could ignite within me. I thought her innocence was what made her so eager to explore. Everything was new to her. She hadn't told me, but I'd known the first time we had sex she'd been a virgin. Maybe not in the technical sense -- women could find alternate means of taking care of that issue if they wanted -- but I'd bet my life she'd never had sex with another man. Might not have even kissed anyone but me. I wasn't stupid enough to point that out, though.

That was a conversation for another day. You know. *After* I'd had time to come up with a phrasing that didn't sound like I thought she was too inexperienced. Right now, the only thing that mattered was Apple, here in this rather austere room, guiding me toward the bed with an impish tug at her lips. Her fingers were warm against mine, her grip firm and promising.

As we approached the bed, she turned and pushed me gently until my knees hit the edge, causing me to sit. She stood between my legs, her hands finding my shoulders to steady herself as she leaned down to kiss me again. The urgency of the moment engulfed us, a fire kindling with every touch and whispered word.

Which was the moment she chose to kneel between my thighs. I nearly shot my load to the ceiling at the sight.

"You really are gonna give me head?"

"Would have the last time if you hadn't been such a bastard." I could see the hurt in her eyes even if she did give me a coquettish grin.

"Show me what I would have gotten if I'd been a good boy." My raspy growl was a direct contrast to my words but I could tell she loved it all. Her skin where she rested her arms on my thighs as she reached for my cock was damp and sticky with sweat. I wanted to collect the moisture by running my tongue over every sweet inch.

Without another word, without ever taking her bright, blue gaze from mine, she lowered her mouth over the head of my cock and down the shaft as much as she could, and sucked.

"Holy Christ!" I gave a sharp shout, my hands going to her head reflexively, my fingers threading in and fisting in the silky gold strands. "What the fuck?" She tried to push back, but there was no way I could move so my hand stayed in her hair. "Don't fuckin' move, Apple." My voice was a husky, strangled growl. "I'm seriously about to blow, so if you want this to continue you need to hold the fuck still!"

Apple's mouth slid down over my cock and the feeling was nothing short of euphoric. She looked up at me through blonde lashes that fluttered softly, her cheeks hollowing out as she took me in farther, then retreated until only the head was in her mouth. Her tongue swirled around the sensitive underside of my shaft, making me hiss. She had to feel how desperate I was for her touch. Now, it was my turn to sweat with need and I realized then, I might be as innocent about love as she was about sex. Because this was most definitely not just sex. I'd fucked countless women. Way more than I wanted to think about. Especially now. But none of them made me feel half of what this one slender, innocent woman was doing now.

Her eyes flickered down to my crotch and then back up to meet my gaze again, a challenge in them. She moved her head slowly, relishing the power she had over me as she began bobbing her head on my shaft to the easier pacing I set with my hands guiding her movements. Up and down, teasing me, driving me wild, yet I couldn't force her to stop altogether. I was incapable of such a move. The warm, wet spit coating her tongue mingled with my pre-cum. I found myself dying to know how sweet the mixture was when I took it straight from her mouth. The thought made me groan loudly.

I tugged her away from my dick and leaned forward to catch her mouth in a kiss, finding out that our combined fluids were, in fact, delicious. My tongue lapped at the inside of her mouth and her tongue. My teeth nipped her delicate lips. I held her that way as I ravished her, claiming her kisses once more before I pulled back to stare down at her. Apple.

"You…" I breathed as I gazed down into her upturned face. "You are my entire world, Apple. There is nothing I wouldn't sacrifice to keep you safe. No one I wouldn't kill."

She gasped, her mouth open and her eyes glazed in her pleasure. She was the one sucking my cock, yet she was enjoying herself as much as I was. "Deacon?"

"Love is too pale a word for how I feel about you." The words were pulled from me, but they felt oddly freeing. I'd said them before, but this time felt different. Maybe because I knew I intended to keep her close to me this time instead of pushing her away.

She smiled up at me as I kept my grip on her hair. She didn't fight my hold, just stared up at me with a lust-filled gaze and a gleam of humor in her eyes. "Very poetic for a badass biker."

I couldn't help the satisfied grin I gave her. "I'll be even more poetic with your mouth back around my cock."

Apple didn't hesitate at all. The moment I let her go, she took my cock back into her mouth, humming as she sank down to take me as deep as she could. When my cock hit the back of her throat, I nearly came. She barely took half of me, but she made good work of as much as she could.

She clenched her fingers into my thighs, her nails digging into my skin. The slight pain grounded me when I wanted nothing more than to lose myself in the moment. That would come later. After I had her writhing beneath me, screaming my name as she came around my cock.

"Enough," I snarled as I pulled her up to kiss her once more. I stood and lifted her, tossing her to the bed and following her. I wedged my shoulders between her legs, then covered her pussy with my mouth.

Apple groaned as I parted her plumped lips, the sound of her cries echoing through the otherwise silent room. Her tangy juices coated my tongue, and I lapped at her clit with relish, tasting her with a greedy hunger. She tasted so fucking good! She writhed under me, crying out in pleasure as she ran her fingers through my hair with one hand and gripped the sheets with the other. She arched her back in invitation.

I let out a low chuckle and moved up the bed to cover her, positioning myself between her legs once more. I couldn't wait to be inside her again, to feel that tight little cunt squeezing me like a glove. She looked up at me, eyes glassy with lust, hands reaching for my shoulders. She pulled me to her, her need and intent clear.

I smiled at her eagerness. "Fuck. Apple," I moaned, hands grasping onto the wooden frame of the bed as I tried to hold on to my control. The last thing I wanted to do was go too fast. I'd suspected her innocence before and had tried to be careful with her. I'd do the same thing this time. I never wanted her to associate sex with pain. Well. Not unless she wanted some pain with her pleasure.

I pushed inside her slowly, feeling the tightness engulf me as she gasped, her pussy squeezing my cock as I glided inside. Her body clenched at my intrusion but Apple welcomed me with a sigh of pleasure that pushed me closer to the edge. "You're so damn perfect," I muttered against her skin as I began to move. "Made for me."

"Deacon!" Apple whimpered as I filled her, her eyes rolled back as she arched in pleasure. When she bucked against me, meeting my strokes with fervor, I growled my praise of her body's acceptance of me. Our mouths crashed together in a hot, desperate kiss.

I ground my hips against hers, needing to put friction against her clit. I was riding the edge of my control, and I'd be damned if I came before her. Her fingers dug into my shoulders again, dragging her nails down my back as she adjusted her grip. Her body was damp with sweat beneath mine, the smell of sex creating an intoxicating mixture with the scent of her freshly washed bedding and her own natural scent.

Her breathing quickened, and I knew she was about to come. When she cried out my name and screamed, her cunt milked me of my own release. My hoarse shout mingled with her cries, and I emptied myself with force as deep in her pussy as I could. I hadn't used a condom and she hadn't insisted. It was a bullshit move, but I'd told her I was making her mine. It was time she realized I absolutely would keep my promise to her. I wanted her with me forever, and I'd do anything I had to, to make it happen.

When we were both spent, I collapsed on top of her, trying my damnedest to catch my breath before I had to look up at her and admit I'd taken her choice from her again. I wasn't sorry. I braced myself for her anger.

"Apple, honey."

"I think you've killed me," she breathed out, then chuckled. "My God, that was spectacular."

I grinned as I kissed the sensitive skin behind her ear. She shivered, holding me to her. Her pussy gave an interested squeeze. My cock responded by trying to harden again. "*You* were spectacular."

"You know, I really shouldn't start a new relationship with you when you're still making decisions for me." She stroked my hair as we lay there.

"Oh? What decision did I make for you, Applejack?" As if I didn't know.

She snorted. "You came inside me. Don't you think that's something we should have discussed?"

"Yeah. But I'm not gonna apologize. I'll never lie to you, and puttin' my cum in this pussy is not something I'll ever be sorry for."

"I'd argue, but the more ties we have weaving us together the better. Besides, if you break up with me again and try to take another woman, I will be petty as shit and make both your lives a living hell. Worse, so will Lemon. And quite possibly Venus."

"You've become good friends with Venus?"

"Good enough. I think she's thinking about asking to join Grim Road. She and Lemon have formed some kind of bond. They help each other."

"Good. Piston says he's claimin' her so that'll work out great for everyone."

"I know. She's putting him off. I thought when they came back from looking for the guy who'd sent men to kidnap Venus they'd have a stronger bond, but if anything she seems to be fighting harder."

"And he's still alive?"

Apple's eyes widened. "Right? See, that's what I thought too! Which means..." We both answered my question at the same time. "She wants him."

We shared a laugh for a few minutes. I kissed her and petted her, praising her for the pleasure she'd given me. Then I pushed off the bed, taking her with me to the bathroom.

I kept my arm around her as I adjusted the water temperature in the shower. Then we both got in and I helped her wash. Then I took her from behind and washed her again.

By the time we tumbled into bed, she was

drooping with exhaustion and more than a little endorphin drop. I held her against my chest, kissing her forehead just so I could feel her soft, smooth skin beneath my lips. Just before I drifted off, I heard my phone buzz again. I knew I needed to take the call, but I just couldn't be bothered at the moment. Whatever it was, it would wait.

Chapter Twelve

Apple

Whoever was banging on my door was gonna die in the most painful way possible. I might not be able to do it myself, but I was pretty sure I could sweet talk Lemon or Venus into doing something horrific.

"What the fuck?" I sat up, covering myself with the sheet.

"Imma kill a motherfucker," Deacon muttered before he kissed the top of my head and got out of bed. He didn't bother to put on pants, just opened the bedroom door and stomped into the living room.

I hastily put on his T-shirt before following him, getting there just as he threw open the door. Naked as the day he was born.

"This better be fuckin' good, Falcon."

"Jesus, man!" Falcon took a couple steps back from Deacon, raising his hands in defense. He also turned his head away and shut his eyes tightly.

I came behind Deacon and wrapped my hand around his bicep. "You might want to put on some pants before you do anything unnatural to him there, babe." I tried to joke, to defuse the situation but, honestly, I was about to laugh until I peed.

"He did this on purpose." Deacon threw me an exasperated look over his shoulder. "Just to piss me off."

"No, bro! I swear! Rocket said he needed you at the clubhouse. I think Crush has something for you on the guy named Calhoun."

Deacon stilled, turning his head slightly as if making sure he'd heard Falcon correctly. "Martin Calhoun? Stepfather of Bear's woman, Olivia?"

"Yeah. That's the bastard."

I sucked in a breath. This was part of the same group of people Deacon had left me to hunt before. Would he do it again? Would I survive if he did? Would Lemon let *him* survive?

"Tell Rocket we'll be there in ten minutes."

"Sorry, man. Apple can't be in on club business. I don't imagine things are any different at Iron Tzars."

"They're not. But Apple goes where I go. Don't like it? Take it up with Lemon."

Falcon stiffened. "Not on your fuckin' life." He backed off another step. "You take it up with Lemon."

Deacon rolled his eyes before slamming the door on Falcon. Then he sighed and knocked his head against the door once. Then again. "Fuck." The word was muttered. Deacon heaved a long sigh. "Just... *fuck.*"

"You have to go." I tried to pretend it didn't hurt he was leaving again, but it did. And it sucked ass.

"Never said that, baby. Let's get dressed, then go see what's goin' on." He turned and pulled me into his arms. "Everything will be all right. I promise."

"Can you make that promise?" I didn't look up at him but buried my face in his chest.

"I can and I am, Apple. I made you a promise and I absolutely will not break it."

"But --"

He cut me off with a kiss. "Don't borrow trouble, Applejack. Trust in me." He gripped my shoulders as he searched my gaze. I could almost feel him willing me to take that leap of faith. It might be foolish, but I knew I was jumping in with both feet.

"You better catch me," I muttered. Instead of asking what I meant, he just grinned at me.

Exactly eight minutes later, we were in Rocket's office. Lemon had, indeed, made the guys let me in. As usual, Rocket merely grinned at his wife with affection like she amused him and, therefore, he'd give her whatever she wanted. Surprisingly, Venus was standing quietly in the corner, Piston stood a few feet away so still and silent he almost seemed to disappear into the background even though he wasn't a small guy.

"If you want to get this guy, now's the time." Crush finished the details of his report. Looked like he and Byte had set something in motion to flush out Martin Calhoun, and it was working. "He'll be on that private island he bought in exactly two weeks. I've arranged for a company called ExFil to take the private detail. ExFil is owned by a guy named Joe Gill who used to be president of Bones MC in Somerset, Kentucky. Pretty sure Iron Tzars has a relationship with him."

"Cain," Deacon said. "His guys gonna take care of the bastard?"

"No. And he's adamant no one should find out about Calhoun's disappearance until several weeks after they pull out. Which is where I come in," Crush continued. "Me and Byte are gonna create some footage to prove Calhoun was out and about right up until everyone forgets ExFil was anywhere near the guy. Cain doesn't want to tarnish the company's reputation by a guy they're protecting getting whacked on their watch."

"Reasonable," Rocket said, stroking his beard. He turned his gaze on me. "Well? This was your baby. What's the next move?"

"I'll get someone from the Tzars to take this. They can take care of business as good as anyone without the wrong people gettin' wind of it."

"Thought you'd be the one goin'." Rocket gave

Deacon a curious look.

"No. I made a promise to Apple I intend to keep. I went back on my word once, and it almost cost me everything, Rocket. Much as I want this kill, I'm not takin' it."

"Suits me." Ringo sat back in his chair. "I'll be happy to take it on."

"Not if I take it first," Bear, Olivia's man, growled at Ringo. "I think I get first dibs on this one."

"I'll take it." Venus moved from where she stood in the corner. "I'll find out everything he knows, and maybe few things he doesn't know he knows."

Rocket raised an eyebrow. "You sure about this? You've been gone from Salvation's Bane for a while. That's your home club. Maybe you better check in with Thorn before you commit to something like this."

Instantly, Venus's expression hardened. "I do what I want. When I want. I'm with Thorn at Bane because he helped me once. He doesn't dictate to me, or tell me what I can or cannot do."

"I'll go with her." Piston shifted just enough to take everyone's attention from Venus and put it squarely on him. "She's Salvation's Bane, so if Thorn has a problem with her takin' this up outside his club, tell him to take it up with me."

"I don't need you to fight my battles, old man." Venus gave Piston an uncharacteristic show of anger and irritation. Usually the woman was as unflappable as they came, but I'd noticed how Piston seemed to get under her skin. Yeah. That was gonna be fun to watch.

"Didn't say you did. But havin' me as a buffer between you and everyone will let you get the job done quicker."

Venus rolled her eyes. "Fine." She pointed her finger at Piston. A finger with a dagger-sharp nail.

Painted hot pink. "Stay out of my way." With that she stomped off. Piston followed her without another word, his expression blank.

There was silence in the room as the two walked out. I glanced at Lemon who had tucked her lips between her teeth, looking for all the world like she was amused.

"We takin' bets on how long Piston lives?" Bear's gaze snapped to Ringo when he spoke, giving the other man a sharp look. Ringo grinned and shrugged. "Just askin'."

"I give it thirty-to-one --" Falcon had a mischievous grin on his face. "-- Dude won't make it through the month."

"Oh, I'll take that action." Lemon laughed. "Hundred bucks."

Falcon's mouth opened in surprise, then his face split in a broad grin. "You're out a hunk of cash, woman. Venus'll eat that fucker alive."

Lemon smirked. "Yep. She sure will. Just not the way you think."

Falcon's smile faded to be replaced by a wary look. Like he sensed a trap but hadn't figured out how to get around it.

"On another note," Crush sighed as he turned around, "I've been looking into Redwood. I should have let it go, but I couldn't. Rocket, he and Hammer were tight. Did some service together overseas they didn't tell anyone about."

"You sayin' they were closer than we knew they were. You think he was bidin' his time until he could get revenge on someone in the club? Me?" His gaze instantly hardened. "Was he going after Lemon to get back at me?" Rocket stiffened, leaned back in his chair, resting one elbow on the armrest as he stroked his chin.

"Hard to say." Crush pushed his glasses up on his nose. "We're all off the books. But, you know if I dig deep enough and hard enough, I can find out anything. If he has someone else out there working with him, we'll find out." Crush scowled, shaking his head.

"You and Byte are invaluable to this club, Crush." Rocket held the man's gaze steadily. "Some of the shit you can do seems like magic."

"Yeah, well, sometimes I wish we weren't so good." He and Byte exchanged a look. Byte winced and turned back to his computer, his shoulders hunching slightly. "I don't know exactly what the op was they went on, but that's when Redwood got involved with the same people Calhoun and Illivitch did business with. I don't know how much Hammer knew, but Redwood was perfectly aware of what he was doing. I'm only guessing -- and I can't stress enough, it's only a guess -- Hammer knew everything Redwood did. What I can't find is anything to link Hammer to the trafficking, but Redwood was in deep."

"Fucker died too easy." Deacon pulled me closer, and I could practically feel the anger vibrating through him.

Crush inhaled a long breath. Held it a couple of seconds, then let it out. "I know I'm the one who vets every single prospect who wants to join us, Rocket. I do it to keep everyone here as safe as I can, but I try not to go past a certain line. Everyone has secrets."

"It's uncomfortable for you." Rocket didn't phrase it as a question.

"Yeah. I accept my responsibilities as the club's tech guy, but I never thought I'd have to spy on my own brothers."

"You're not spying," Lemon moved to stand behind Crush. She put a hand on his shoulder. "You're keeping everyone safe. Including the people you look into. Besides, it's not like you share anything with anyone. You tell Rocket anything you think he needs to know. The rest goes in a file only you, Byte, and Rocket have access to. He can read it if he wants, but unless you tell him to look at something, he respects everyone's privacy."

No one in the room looked uncomfortable but Crush and Byte. Despite some pretty major setbacks, these guys had stuck together and started opening up to each other more than when I'd first met them. Which was mostly all Lemon's doing. My sister was a force of nature when she decided she wanted something, and she wanted Grim Road to be a family. Slowly but surely, she was achieving her goal. All thanks to her.

"Was anyone else tight with Redwood or Hammer?" Rocket drew the attention back to him.

"Not that I've found," Crush said. "I don't expect to find anything. 'Course, I didn't expect what happened with Redwood either."

"No one did, Crush." Rocket turned his attention to Deacon. "So? You're letting Venus take point on this. You headin' back to Iron Tzars?"

Deacon shrugged. "Don't know." He glanced down at me. "I suppose I'll go wherever Apple goes, so maybe you should ask her."

That startled me. "You really meant what you said before? You'd leave Iron Tzars if I wanted to stay here?"

"I meant it when I said I wasn't leaving you again. That means I go where you go. I want you happy so if you want to stay here, I'll put in whatever formal request Rocket wants for me to patch over to Grim Road."

I looked at Lemon who gave me a smirk and nodded her head. I smiled at my sister. My twin. I loved Dani just as much as Lemon, but it was different. Lemon was part of me. The months we'd been apart when she first came to Grim Road had been the longest of my life.

"I'm not ready to leave my sister again," I said softly. "I'm sorry, Deacon. I don't want to make things difficult for you, but I want to stay here."

"Then that's what you'll do. It took an act of God and the promise of my firstborn for Rocket to let me in here in the first place, so I've got motivation to stay." He grinned, giving me an affectionate look. "Truth is, I'd rather you stay here until Venus does her thing and rids the world of Martin Calhoun. I wasn't lying when I told you I thought Grim was the safest place for you to be."

"You can use the time to suck up to me, Deacon." Lemon gave Deacon a bright smile. Which always meant she was getting ready to wreak havoc on some unsuspecting mortal. In this case, it was definitely Deacon.

Deacon only grinned. "I'll look forward to it. Sister."

That wiped the smile off Lemon's face in a hurry. "No way. You might be with my sister, but that in no way makes you my brother."

"Always wanted a little sister. I'll tie your hair in knots and put worms in your bed."

"And I'll put Nair in your shampoo and give your bike a brand-new paint job."

"Oh, hell no," Knox said, sitting up straighter in his seat. "No more fuckin' pink bikes in my fuckin' garage, Lemon. There's a line."

"And you know I just love obliterating those pesky boundaries, Knox. So, suck it up, buttercup."

"I'm gettin' too old for this shit." Knox stood. "Rocket, if you don't need me any longer, I've got to go do something to forget about the two pink Harleys that I can't trash sitting in my garage."

Rocket waved Knox on, chuckling as he did. "Never a dull moment in this place, Deacon. You'd make a good addition."

"Let's wait 'til Venus comes back. Me and Apple'll hash it out, then let you know." It both shocked and thrilled me that he included me in the decision. Maybe he was learning from his mistakes after all.

"You know," I spoke up, needing to point out the obvious. "Y'all mentioned Venus coming back several times, but you haven't said a thing about Piston."

"That's because she'll probably kill him before he has a chance to come back."

"I'm tellin' you, Falcon," Lemon said, "Piston'll win her over. I think he already has and she's just playing hard to get."

"Don't think that just because you're the VP you can renege on your bet. When I win, you're gonna owe me a pretty penny."

"And when I win, I'm going to enjoy that hundred dollars. Might frame it and put it above the bar in the common room. I'll put a plaque on it that says, 'Proof Lemon is always right'."

I gazed up at Deacon and, for the first time, had some real hope for our future. It was small things like telling Rocket we'd discuss where we wanted to stay as well as big things like not going back out on the hunt in order to keep his promise and stay with me. I could tell, looking into his eyes, he was at peace with his decision. It wasn't something he was giving up for me. The man truly didn't want to leave me.

"I feel like I already won." The words slipped out quietly. I wasn't sure if anyone else heard me, but Deacon did. His gaze softened as he looked down at me.

"Me too, Applejack. Me too."

Because he was trying, I thought I needed to try too. "You know, if it's something you really want to do, Deacon, you can go after Calhoun. Just promise to come back and to not shut me out again. That's all I need." I sucked in a breath at the thought of him leaving. "I can't lose you again, Deacon." We were still in Rocket's office with people around us, but our conversation was quiet. Between us only. It struck me that it didn't matter. These people were as much my family as the guys at Iron Tzars. I knew everyone here had my back.

"I'm doing exactly what I want, Apple. I'm not OK with being away from you. Not any more than absolutely necessary. There's plenty of people in both Grim and Tzars willin' to do this. Ain't sayin' I'll never have to leave for short periods of time, but I promise I will always come back to you."

That must have been exactly what I needed to hear because a band around my chest loosened. I hadn't realized how worried I'd been until that very moment. The relief was nearly overwhelming, and I found the room spinning slightly. Then Deacon wrapped his arms around me and held me tightly against him.

"Get a room, you two." Lemon laughed cheerfully. "Rocket, let's me and you get a room too. I feel the need to get freaky."

"Far be it from me to go against my vice president's wishes."

"I want to get freaky too," Deacon whispered.

"Yes," I said, nodding my head emphatically. I couldn't help the big cheesy grin on my face. "Let's do that."

Deacon took me back home. Once inside he stripped me bare. I laughed and ran from him only to let him catch me in the backyard. And yeah. We were both bare-assed naked. When he finally caught me, he laid me down on a bed of soft clover, covering me with his body and making love to me under the warm sunshine. Everything might not be perfect, but I could honestly say I could never remember being more content. I had Deacon. He had me. We had each other. Life was better than good.

Life was... *beautiful.*

Marteeka Karland

International bestselling author Marteeka Karland leads a double life as an action romance writer by evening and a semi-domesticated housewife by day. Known for her down-and-dirty MC romances, Marteeka takes pleasure in spinning tales of tenacious, protective heroes and spirited heroines. She staunchly advocates that every character deserves a blissful ending.

Marteeka finds joy in baking, and gardening with her husband. Make sure to visit her website to stay updated with her most recent projects. Don't forget to register for her newsletter which will pepper you with a potpourri of Teeka's beloved recipes, book suggestions, autograph events, and a plethora of interesting tidbits.

Series reading order for Iron Tzars MC

More books by Marteeka Karland
Want more? Find Teeka's Dark Erotica side here: Wanda Violet O.

Bones MC Multiverse

Bones MC
Shadow Demons
Salvation's Bane MC
Black Reign MC
Iron Tzars MC
Grim Road MC
Bones MC Legends
Bones MC Audio
Salvation's Bane MC Audio
Iron Tzars MC Audio
Bones MC Print Duets

Changeling Press, LLC

ChangelingPress.com